THE SECRETS OF DROON

Volume II

by Tony Abbott

Illustrated by Tim Jessell

SCHOLASTIC INC.
New York Toronto London Auckland Sydney
Mexico City New Delhi Hong Kong Buenos Aires

The Great Ice Battle, ISBN 0-590-10843-3.
Text copyright © 1999 by Robert T. Abbott. Illustrations copyright © 1999 by Scholastic Inc. Book design by Dawn Adelman.

The Sleeping Giant of Goll, ISBN 0-590-10844-1.
Copyright © 2000 by Robert T. Abbott. Book design by Dawn Adelman.

Into the Land of the Lost, ISBN 0-439-18297-2.
Text copyright © 2000 by Robert T. Abbott. Illustrations copyright © 2000 by Scholastic Inc. Book design by Dawn Adelman.

The Golden Wasp, ISBN 0-439-18298-0.
Copyright © 2000 by Robert T. Abbott. Book design by Dawn Adelman.

12 11 10 9 8 7 6 5 4 3 2 1   5 6 7 8 9 10/0

Printed in the U.S.A.   40

This edition created exclusively for Barnes & Noble, Inc.

2005 Barnes & Noble Books

ISBN 0-7607-9540-1

First compilation printing, May 2005

Contents

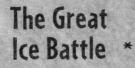

The Great
Ice Battle

To Dolores,
without whom none
of this would be

Contents

One

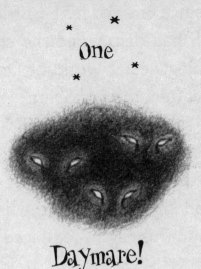

Daymare!

As cold as ice.

That's how Eric Hinkle felt as he jumped from his bed.

"Brrr!" he said to himself, shivering. He pulled on his thick socks. He got into his warmest winter pants. He shivered again. Eric was having bad thoughts of an evil sorcerer. And that's what was giving him the creeps — but not why he was so cold.

Ever since Eric and his best friends, Julie and Neal, had discovered the entrance to the amazing, secret world of Droon, they had been afraid of Lord Sparr.

"Who wouldn't be afraid?" Eric said aloud.

With those creepy purple fins growing up behind his ears. And the long black cloak. And his ugly red-faced warriors called Ninns.

Sparr was the reason Eric felt so cold.

The evil sorcerer wanted only one thing.

To take over all of Droon.

"But now, things in Droon are different," Eric said as he dug in his closet for his winter coat.

On their last adventure in Droon, Sparr had had a chance to hurt Eric. But he hadn't done it.

He had let him live. He'd said Eric would *help* him.

"I'll never help you!" Eric said with a shudder.

"Why won't you help me?"

"Because you're evil!" Eric snapped back.

"Eric!"

He blinked. His father was standing in the doorway to his room. He was frowning.

"Dad!" Eric said. "I'm sorry. You're not evil. I guess I was daydreaming or something."

His father sighed. "Well, you can help me later. Neal and Julie are waiting for you outside."

"Thanks!" Eric threw on his coat and ran downstairs to the back door. Still shivering, he grabbed his cap, pulled it low over his eyes, and wrapped his scarf tight around his neck.

He flung open the door. "Whoa!" he gasped.

Warm air and bright sunshine poured in.

Julie and Neal were dressed in T-shirts and shorts. They had a softball, mitts, and a bat.

"It's not hockey season!" Neal said, chuckling.

Julie made a face. "Are you okay, Eric?"

He stared at his friends. Then he tore off his coat and scarf. "This is sooooo weird! I was cold. I was freezing! I must have daydreamed that it was winter! Sorry."

Julie tossed the ball up. "So, who's pitching?"

"Me first!" Neal grabbed the ball from Julie.

"No, me!" said Eric.

"Sorry, pal. I called it," said Neal. "Besides, I've got this new throw to show you! I just twist my fingers and shoot the ball. It's fast!"

Eric took the bat, but in his mind he kept seeing Lord Sparr.

"Why don't we use *ice* today?" Sparr was saying.

Ice. That was the other thing Sparr had said the last time they were in Droon. Sparr was going to do something bad with ice.

"We'll defeat Princess Keeah," the Sparr in Eric's mind continued. "And the old wizard, Galen. You will help me. . . ."

"No way!" Eric cried, dropping the bat. "I'll never do it! Never!"

"Are you going to play or not?" Neal said.

Eric turned to his friends. "Sorry, guys. But something weird is going on. I keep

seeing Sparr in my mind. He's telling me how I'm going to help him. It's like a nightmare, only it's daytime."

"A daymare!" Julie said. Then she gasped. "Wait a second. Do you think the daydreams mean we need to go to Droon?"

Their friend Princess Keeah had told them that when they dreamed about Droon, it meant the magic was working.

It meant they needed to return.

Eric nodded slowly. "This might be some kind of message or something." He started for the back steps. "We need to re-turn. Now."

"What? No!" Neal jumped up and down. "I need to show you my new twisty throw — hey!"

But Julie and Eric were already in the house.

"Oh, man!" said Neal. "I knew we weren't going to play this game. I just knew it!"

By the time Neal caught up with them, Eric and Julie were halfway down the basement stairs.

"We'll play when we get back," Julie said. "It's not as if Droon takes any time. No matter how long our adventure is, we come back around the same time we left. It's so neat that way."

This was true. One of the very coolest things the kids discovered was that it took no time at all to have a full adventure in Droon.

"Time is strange there," Eric said. "It's different from here in the Upper World."

The Upper World was Droon's name for where the kids lived.

Neal set the softball on the workbench. Julie and Eric pushed aside a large box.

Behind it was the door to a small empty room under the basement stairs.

Carefully, they went inside the room. Eric closed the door behind them. Julie clicked off the light.

For an instant the room was dark, then —

Whoosh! A set of rainbow-colored stairs appeared where the floor used to be.

"I love that!" Julie whispered.

Eric took the first step. "Let's go."

They began their descent.

"I can't see anything but the stairs," Eric whispered. "It's totally dark all around."

Julie took a deep breath. "Do you think the stairs can lead us to someplace bad?"

"Thanks for scaring me," Neal mumbled, clutching the stair rail.

"I'm not sure," said Eric. "I guess that's one of Droon's many secrets — whoa!"

"What is it?" asked Neal, huddling closer.

"That was the bottom step," said Eric.

No sooner had they stepped off than the stairway began to fade. A moment later, it was gone.

"No turning back now," said Julie.

They stepped forward. Eric stuck his hands out. "I think it's some kind of cave. The walls are rough. So is the floor. Be careful."

"It smells like animals," Julie added.

Grrrr!

Everyone stopped.

"Is somebody going to say 'Excuse me,' or are we in deep trouble?" Neal asked.

Grrrr! The growling noise was closer this time.

"I hear breathing," Julie whispered.

"And I s-s-see . . . eyes!" Neal stammered. "Red eyes! Lots of them!"

Eric shivered again, then whispered, "Everyone who agrees we should run, say 'Run.'"

"RUN!" they all cried.

They ran.

Two

City of Light

The three friends scrambled through the cave as fast as they could.

Grrr! Grrr! Whatever was behind them was following swiftly.

"There's light up ahead!" Julie called back.

"I'm there!" said Neal.

"Last one out is a rotten egg!" Eric cried.

They hurled themselves out of the mouth of the cave and into the light. Bright light. And green grass. And flowers. They tripped over a low wall and tumbled down a short slope to a wire fence.

"We're trapped!" Neal yelled.

Suddenly, the kids heard laughter.

They sat up and squinted through the fence.

Standing behind it were Princess Keeah and her father, King Zello.

"Welcome to Droon!" the king boomed.

They looked back at the cave. The red eyes blinked and disappeared into the darkness.

Eric jumped to his feet. "You mean . . . we're safe?"

"Very," Keeah said with a giggle. "You just looked funny running out of the wolves' cave."

Neal gulped. "Did you say . . . *wolves?* Man, I hope we never go back into that cave!"

Keeah and her father opened an iron gate and helped the three kids outside the fence.

"The red wolves of Droon are famous," King Zello said. "They protect our city!"

The king was a tall man with broad shoulders. He wore a helmet with horns and carried a wooden club. Princess Keeah had long blonde hair. She wore a green tunic and leather boots.

"Welcome to Jaffa City," Keeah said. "Jaffa is the royal city of Droon!"

The princess led them out to a stone courtyard that was larger than a baseball stadium.

At one side was a busy marketplace. Men and women strolled and shopped at colorful tents. Their children played happily by a beautiful fountain nearby.

"Wow," said Eric. "I had bad daydreams

about Sparr. But things look pretty okay here!"

On the other side of the square rose giant buildings of white and silver and green and pink stone. In between grew flowers and bushes, and birds sang in white-blossomed apple trees.

A soft breeze blew across the vast open space.

"It sure is beautiful," Julie said as they passed the fountain. The children of Droon waved to the three friends from the Upper World.

"Friendly, too," Neal said, giving the kids the peace sign.

"And someday Keeah will rule over this city as well as all the villages outside," the king said. "Just like her mother, Queen Relna."

Keeah's mother was a wizard who had

been transformed into a white falcon. In that shape, she had helped the kids fight Lord Sparr. Now she herself needed help to become human again.

"But for now, Keeah," the king said, "you must get ready for your magic lessons. Galen will be here soon. Max will come, too, of course."

Galen was a powerful old wizard. Max was his spider-troll assistant.

The king beamed with pride and said, "Galen tells me that in some ways Keeah's powers are greater than his own. When the time is right, her true powers will be revealed."

Eric's eyes went wide. "Powers? Cool!"

Keeah made a face. "More like lukewarm. So far, I've broken seven clay pots, one bowl, a chair, and two clocks."

"Three clocks," her father said, smiling.

"But Galen will teach you. And look, here he comes!"

A thick blue mist rose in the middle of the square. Sparks of light streaked through it.

An instant later — *zamm*! A bearded old man in a long blue robe stood there. Next to him sat a large spider with four arms and four legs. He had a round face, a pug nose, and orange hair that stood straight up.

"Galen! Max!" Eric said. "Good to see you again!"

But the wizard did not look happy.

"What's wrong?" the king asked, gripping his wooden club tightly.

There was fear in Max's eyes as he spoke. "Terrible!" he chittered. "Lord Sparr! He's coming!"

"I fear the worst," Galen said. "A curse

has been sent by the evil one. We've tracked it across the plains. Now look!"

Galen pointed to the skies above them. A vast black cloud passed quickly in front of the sun. The entire courtyard fell into shadow.

"It is a curse!" Max muttered.

Eric thought of his daydream again. He shivered with cold as he shot a look at Keeah.

"What kind of curse?" he asked.

A snowflake fell from the darkening sky. Another followed it. Then another and another.

The sun vanished completely. The air grew icy cold. Freezing wind tore across the city.

The trees that had been so beautiful were instantly crusted with heavy frost.

Ice formed on the city walls and on the stones of the courtyard.

Eric remembered what Sparr had said.

"Ice!" he cried, shivering. "Sparr is using ice to attack us! It's just like he told me!"

Keeah's eyes went wide with fear. "Oh, my Jaffa City!"

Three

White Snow, Dark Magic

Within moments the city was covered with ice. Biting winds swirled snow into huge drifts.

"This is Sparr's dark magic!" Galen said.

Crrrack! The fountain's silvery stream thickened and suddenly went still.

"This is just like my daydream," Eric said. "It's a curse of ice."

The colorful banners over the marketplace stopped waving. Icicles formed on the buildings and hung like daggers over the frozen streets.

Eric saw the fear in Keeah's eyes. He shivered, too. "What can we do to stop this?"

Keeah turned to the king. "Our villages can't survive this cold. We must save our people!"

Zello nodded. "I shall go help the villagers. Keeah, you stay here and keep Jaffa City safe. Galen, I must go quickly. Perhaps your latest invention . . ."

"Ah!" the wizard said. "My water sled. Yes, it should ride quite well on ice. Follow me!" Galen led the king and his guards to the stables.

"We'll help, too!" Neal said, clapping his arms around himself. "If we don't fr-fr-freeze f-first!"

Max scuttled over. "Let me make you

warm!" he chirped. "I'll spin you coats of my special spider silk. It's the warmest fabric in all of Droon!"

Max's arms and legs began to blur in the air all around the kids. Soon, he had woven each one a thick coat and a pair of furry boots.

"Thank you," said Julie. "They're very warm."

A moment later, several shaggy six-legged beasts called pilkas trotted across the square to the gate.

In the lead was Leep, Galen's own pet pilka.

Behind them, the pilkas dragged a sleek wooden sled. It looked like a small boat and rode over the ice on long skis. King Zello, bundled in a cloak of bright blue fur, was riding in the back.

"Be careful!" Keeah said, hugging her father.

"I shall be. And you, too," he replied.

Errrr! Two guards pushed aside a large bolt and the city's huge iron gates swung open.

The king snapped the reins, and Leep charged ahead, pulling Galen's sled into the swirling snow.

Keeah waved one last time before — *clong!* — the gates closed.

"I predict he will be safe," Galen said.

Neal frowned. "But, um, what about us? Could Sparr just march in here with his Ninns?"

Keeah beamed. "Galen charmed our walls! An evil spirit can't enter unless he is invited."

"That is true," the wizard said. "An old spell."

"And we never *will* invite evil ones into Jaffa!" Max chittered. "They have no manners!"

"Excellent," said Neal. "I like being safe for a change."

Keeah smiled. "Now, everyone, come. Let's get warm in the throne room!"

Julie and Neal hurried in after Keeah. The guards went with Galen into the frosted palace. Max scuttled across the stones after his master.

But Eric stayed behind for a moment. He climbed to the top of the wall and looked out. The nearby villages were quickly being swallowed up by the deep snow.

He shuddered. But it wasn't from the cold.

Did I make this happen somehow? he wondered. *Did I already help Sparr do this? How?*

"No! I couldn't have done this!" he shouted into the storm. "And I won't help Sparr, either! Never! Ever!"

He turned to go into the palace.

"Help!" a tiny voice cried out.

Eric looked down. The courtyard below was empty of everything but ice and snow.

"Help!" the voice called out again.

Eric looked back over the wall. There, in the deepening snow, was a small figure. A boy.

The boy shivered in thin clothes, his tiny arms wrapped around him. He looked just like the children playing in the square before.

"Help me!" the boy pleaded. "I was playing. I got left outside."

Eric turned to the gates. "Guards!" he yelled.

But the guards had gone inside with Galen.

The only sound was the red wolves starting to howl from their cave.

The little boy trembled even more.

"Wait a second! Hold on!" Eric yelled. He ran down the steps to the front gate.

He could hear the child whimpering outside. "Wait!" Eric called. With all his strength he pushed the gate's huge bolt aside. Then he dug his feet into the snow and pulled on the giant door. It wouldn't budge. He pulled harder.

Finally, it opened a tiny crack.

Eric peered into the swirling winds. Ice pelted his face. "Where are you?" he shouted.

The wolves howled again.

So did the wind.

"Cold!" the boy said. He stood a few feet from the iron door, the storm whipping at his ragged clothes. He was nearly covered in ice.

"So cold!" the boy groaned.

"Come in!" Eric cried, reaching for the boy. "Get warm inside!"

The boy leaped past Eric. He was through the gates in a single bound.

"Thank you," the boy said. Then he turned and looked Eric straight in the eye. He grinned.

"I told you that you would help me!" he said.

Eric gasped. "What do you mean? Wait . . . no . . . no!"

The wolves howled a final time.

And the boy's face began to change.

Four

A Party of Evil Dudes

The small boy's pale skin turned the color of ashes. Then he wiggled and stretched himself up to the size of a tall man.

"No . . . no . . ." Eric mumbled. "It can't be!"

The figure's narrow shoulders broadened. His rags fell away to reveal a long black cloak. But the worst part was the purple fins that sprouted behind his ears.

"Sparr is here!" Eric cried. "Help!"

He raced as fast as he could to the palace.

Galen ran down the steps. A dozen armed guards dashed out with him. "Eric, what is it?"

"I messed up! I messed up big-time!" Eric said, falling to the steps, his heart racing with fear. "Sparr tricked me! I let him in! I helped him!"

Neal, Julie, and Keeah rushed to Eric.

"Hide, all of you," the wizard said sharply, striding out to the courtyard. "Guards, come!"

The four kids crept out as far as they could, then ducked behind a tall snowdrift. Max skittered out of the palace and huddled with them.

"How stupid could I be?" Eric groaned softly.

Lord Sparr stood by the gate. His deep

eyes flickered and blazed red. His transformation was complete.

"Seize him!" Galen called out. A dozen of the king's soldiers quickly surrounded Sparr.

The sorcerer bared his teeth in an evil grin. "How rude to treat an invited guest with such . . . coldness!" His fingers sparked suddenly.

"Galen, watch out!" Keeah cried. She raised her own hand. A beam of pale light shot from it.

It fizzled and vanished in an instant.

Blam! Sparr's bolt struck the wizard. Galen was thrown backward in the snow.

Then he stopped moving.

His blue robe went stiff. His long white hair and beard turned to ice. Frost crept over his cheeks, his forehead, his nose.

"Oh, Galen!" Max whimpered. "No . . . no . . ."

The wizard's eyes went glassy. "So cold!" he said. Then he said no more.

Before the guards could move — *kkkk!* Another bolt of light shot from Sparr. The guards turned to ice as quickly as Galen had.

The wolves howled deep in their cave. Sparr smiled. "Yes, even you shall fall to my curse."

Kkkk! Blam! The wolves howled no more.

"We've got to stop this guy!" Eric whispered.

Boom-boom-boom! There came a loud knocking on the gates. Sparr turned. With a flick of his wrist, the gates opened. "Come, my Ninns!"

"Oh, great!" Neal groaned. "Now he's inviting his Ninns in, too! A regular party of evil dudes!"

Twenty of Sparr's heavy-footed, red-faced Ninn warriors clomped into the courtyard.

Some of them carried huge hammers over their shoulders. Others had bows and arrows.

They grunted and bowed before their master.

"You four, bring me the amulet of Zor," the sorcerer commanded.

"Yes, Lord Sparr," growled the chief Ninn.

"You three, take the old wizard to the throne room," Sparr said. "The rest of you, find the children. The boy helped me get in. But his usefulness is done. Now, destroy them all!"

Sparr swirled his cloak and swept up the steps into the palace.

The children quaked with fear.

"Keeah," whispered Julie. "You must know a spell against this. Don't you have some magic that will unfreeze the wizard?"

Keeah hung her head. "My magic failed when I needed it most." Her tears fell to the ground and turned to ice.

"Don't despair, princess," Max whispered. "Galen will be fine. At least . . . I hope he will!"

"Well, there's got to be something we can do," said Eric.

Neal turned to Eric. "A . . ."

"A what?" Eric asked. "You have an idea?"

"A . . . a . . ." Neal said, shivering.

"Tell us!" Julie whispered.

"A . . . a . . . *choo*!" Neal sneezed loudly.

"Huh?" grunted one of the Ninns in the courtyard. He pointed to the drift where the kids were hiding. "Snow . . . sneeze?"

"Not snow! Little ones!" shouted an-other.

The Ninns loaded their bows and ar-rows.

"That's our cue to get out of here!" Julie said.

"Let's hide in the market," Keeah said. "We can lose the Ninns there!"

"Better than losing our lives *here*!" Neal said.

The five friends bolted up in a swirl of snow and took off across the courtyard.

The angry Ninns clomped right after them!

Five

The Gift of Magic

Thwang! Thwang!

Arrows whizzed past the kids as they dashed across the snowy courtyard. The arrows plinked and clanked against the frosted stones.

"Head for the rows of market stalls!" Keeah said, pointing ahead. "We can hide there!"

Max skittered on the stones behind

Keeah. "Oh, if only my master, Galen, were here!"

They darted into the thick of the marketplace. The tents were crusted with snow and ice. Men and women stood by their tables. But they weren't moving. They were completely frozen.

"This is so sad," said Julie, out of breath.

"I know them," Keeah added.

Clomp! Crash! The Ninns burst through the first row of stalls searching for the kids. They tore down the tents and overturned the tables.

"Oh, dear!" Max chittered. "Terrible brutes!"

"I agree!" said Eric, hurrying past a stall filled with barrels of sugar and flour.

Clomp! Ninns were storming around from behind. Soon they would see the kids.

"Ninn sandwich!" Neal said. "We're trapped!"

"I've got an idea!" Eric whispered. Then he grabbed Neal and pushed his face into one of the sugar barrels.

"Hey!" Neal yelped, pulling himself back up, his face covered with white sugar. "What are you doing? I mean — mmm. That's good sugar."

"Shhh!" Eric gasped. "Pretend you're frozen!"

"Huh?" Then Neal's eyes went wide. "Oh, I get it! The sugar looks like frost!" He went stiff.

Julie and Keeah got the idea, too. They stuck their faces in the sugar barrel, then popped back up. They stood as still as statues.

Eric did the same. So did Max.

Their faces were completely frosted in sugar.

They held their breaths.

Clomp! Clank! Two red Ninns in black armor stomped between the stalls to the children.

"Child?" growled one. He poked one of his six claws at Neal's nose. He waved the other in front of Eric's face. Both boys stared straight ahead. They didn't move. They didn't breathe.

"Frozen?" the Ninn said.

The other Ninn peered at Keeah. Then he pushed his big red face down close to Julie's. His dark, beady eyes stared into hers.

"Frozen," he grunted to his fellow Ninn.

They wandered away noisily between the stalls. Finally they headed back to the palace.

Eric let out a long breath. "That was close!"

"Real close," Neal said, brushing the sugar from his cheeks. "I never knew food could save your life!"

"Let's get out of here," said Julie. "Before that big lug decides to breathe on me again —"

"Shhh!" Keeah said. "I hear something."

The kids stood still and listened.

Eric looked up. "It sounds like . . . wings!"

"It's Queen Relna!" Max exclaimed. "Look!"

Down through the swirling snow came a white falcon. She fluttered slowly above them.

"Mother!" the princess said softly.

"Keeah, my child," the falcon said. "How I can speak to you, I do not know. But Keeah . . . only you have the power to save our city."

"My magic failed!" Keeah replied. "I

couldn't help Galen. I tried to, but Sparr froze him!"

"And it's all my fault," Eric muttered.

The bird spoke again. "Sometimes bad things happen for a reason. We need to be tested, so that we grow stronger. Keeah, remember who you are. And know this: True magic comes from a magic heart."

Then the bird hovered over the barrel of sugar. From her eyes came a spiral of blue light.

The light fell on the sugar. The sugar began to sparkle.

"Hurry!" said the queen. "You have but a little time left before what is frozen remains frozen!"

Then, with a rapid flutter of wings, Keeah's mother was gone.

"Wow, is that magic dust?" Julie asked.

Eric remembered how Keeah had once

sprinkled shiny powder on his sprained ankle, curing him.

The princess tossed a handful of the sparkling crystals in the air and watched them fall. "I think it is magic," she said.

"Then let's get to the palace right away and try the dust on Galen," Eric said.

"Excuse me," Neal said, raising his hand. "But Sparr is in there, with a million nasty Ninns."

"Neal's right," Keeah said. She filled a velvet pouch on her belt with the powder. "We'll need some help first."

"Good thinking!" Neal said. He dipped his finger in the barrel of sugar and licked it. "Mmm. It's magic, but it still tastes good."

Eric turned to Keeah. "Should we wait here for your father to get back with an army of big, tough Droon guys?"

Keeah shook her head. "We can't wait. We need other friends to help us. Old friends."

Neal gulped. "Hold on a second. You're not talking about those wolves, are you?"

Keeah patted her velvet pouch. "We need to unfreeze them."

"You *are* talking about those wolves!" Neal yelped. "Oh, man! I knew we were going back to that cave! I just knew it!"

The princess had already grabbed Julie and Eric and started to run.

"To the cave, everyone!" she cried. "Hurry!"

Six

The Red Wolves of Droon

"It's like a tomb in here," Eric said as they entered the cave. "And darker than I remember it."

"Thanks for scaring me again," said Neal.

Keeah pulled a flaming torch from the wall outside and handed it to Max. She took another for herself. "It gets even darker down below."

Carefully, the five friends tiptoed into

the darkness. Soon, the rocky cave floor gave way to rough, carved steps.

Sssss! The torches sizzled as the thick ice on the ceiling melted down onto the flames.

Eric felt bad about letting Sparr in. There was nothing he could do now, except help make it right. He hoped they could reverse the curse.

"How did the wolves get here?" he asked.

Keeah stepped carefully down the frosted steps. "Long ago, a terrible creature named Zor fought the wolves who lived in the hills here."

"Who is Zor?" asked Julie.

Keeah took a deep breath. "He was a giant."

"A terrible giant! If the stories are to be believed," Max said with a shiver.

"My mother took the giant's power

away," Keeah said. "He vanished. Finally, he died."

Max nodded. "To thank Relna, the wolves promised to guard forever the amulet that gave Zor his power."

"What's an amulet?" Neal asked.

"A kind of crest," Keeah said. "A big piece of jewelry with a crystal in the center. It's hidden below our city, in the cavern of the wolves."

"So that's what Sparr is after!" Eric said.

Julie frowned. "But if Zor is dead, what exactly will Sparr do with the giant's old jewelry?"

"I don't know," Keeah whispered. "But something tells me we'll find out soon enough."

They stepped off the final step onto a smooth floor. Before them was an opening into a stone room. Beyond that was an even smaller room.

"Oh, no!" Julie gasped. "The poor wolves!"

There, in the flickering torchlight, were three large wolves.

One lay motionless near the entrance to the inner room. Another was standing on all fours, its long ears pointed up, its eyes as still as glass. A third crouched by the stairs, its fangs bared, as if ready to pounce. The bright red fur of each wolf was now silvery-white with ice.

All three were frozen solid.

"Just like my master," Max chirped softly.

"According to the old stories, there was only one thing that could stop them," Keeah said.

"Let me guess. Being frozen," Eric said. "And that's why Sparr used a curse of ice to attack the city. He knew he could get Zor's amulet."

"He already did," Julie said. She pointed to the inner room. It was empty.

Neal joined her and gazed up. "There's a hole in the ceiling here. The Ninns must have busted their way in with those nasty hammers."

Max shot sticky silk at the ceiling and swung up to the hole. "I'll see what I can find out."

Keeah took a deep breath and opened her velvet bag. She sprinkled powder on the wolves.

Zzzz! The air sizzled over the frozen beasts.

"It's working!" Eric said. "The magic is working!"

The creatures' eyes softened instantly.

One wolf yawned and stretched. The others shook themselves from head to tail, spraying a thousand icy needles across the stones.

"Yes!" Julie cried. "They're alive!"

Keeah knelt and whispered to the red wolves. *"Sama teku mey?"* The animals seemed to answer her with purring sounds and soft growling.

She has the power, Eric thought. He glanced at his friends. Their eyes were wide with wonder.

Keeah turned back to the kids. "I must help Galen. Even if it means facing Sparr. I must trust the magic. That's what my mother's words mean."

"Her words mean something to us, too," Eric agreed.

Max swung back into the room. "Those nasty Ninns are taking Zor's amulet to the throne room. Sparr is waiting for it there."

Keeah's eyes flashed. "The king's room? Only my father should sit there!"

The wolves growled, sensing Keeah's anger.

"We'll bring your father back," said Eric. "We'll make things right again. We have to."

Julie nodded. "We'll do it."

"We make a great team," Neal added.

Keeah smiled. "Then come. We have work to do!"

Seven

A Royal Wizard

They climbed up a secret passage and came out a small door on the main level of the palace.

Max peered around in all directions. "No Ninns," he chirped. "As long as we're quiet!"

"The throne room is not far from here," Keeah said. "Everybody, follow me."

Eric crept close to the frosty walls. Julie

and Neal were right behind him. The red wolves padded silently next to Keeah.

Soon they were outside the throne room.

Eric and Neal peered around one side of the doorway, Julie and Keeah around the other.

The throne room was large and round. The walls were covered with tapestries. The floor was tiled in a strange pattern of colored stones.

Eric had seen that pattern before, in Galen's secret tower. The throne room's floor was a giant map of Droon.

Sparr sat in the king's large golden throne.

Galen stood nearby, as white and unmoving as a statue carved of stone.

"Bring the amulet to me!" Sparr commanded.

Grrr! The wolves growled behind Keeah.

"Hush!" she said, patting their heads. "Soon."

Four big Ninn soldiers carried an iron box into the room. They set it down in front of their master, opened the box, and bowed.

With both hands Sparr reached in and pulled out a large black object. He held it over his head.

It was a long triangle piercing a circle. Horns stuck out from either side.

A glittering crystal hung in the center of the triangle.

"Behold the amulet of Zor!" Sparr cried out.

The Ninns bowed before the strange object.

The amulet sparkled in the torchlight.

"Soon, we shall begin our long journey," Sparr announced. "Zor . . . we shall come to you!"

"Oh, dear!" Max whispered.

Then Lord Sparr drew his sword. He attached the amulet to the handle and tightened it.

"What is he doing?" Julie asked.

Keeah frowned. "I don't know."

The sorcerer strode to the center of the room.

He stood over the spot where the colored tiles showed the outline of Jaffa City. "Soon our questions will be answered," he said.

He clutched his sword with both hands.

He pointed the blade down.

With one powerful thrust — *clong!* — Sparr sank his blade deep into the floor.

Deep into the map of Jaffa City.

"What is going on —" Eric began.

Suddenly, the amulet's crystal lit up. It began glowing bright green. It sparked and hissed.

Keeah stood up. "It's time," she said.

"We'll bring back the king," Eric said firmly.

The princess took a deep breath. "Good luck."

"To you, too," said Julie, smiling at her.

Keeah stepped from the shadows. *"Detchu-tah!"* she called out sharply.

In a flash, the three large red wolves roared into the throne room. They growled and bared their fangs. Steam rose from their open jaws as they skittered by Keeah's side.

Sparr stepped back. Fear crossed his face. "The wolves? They were frozen! So . . . you *are* your mother's daughter. Too bad your little show of magic won't last very long."

"Long enough to stop you!" Keeah said. She raised her hands at Sparr.

Eric felt his blood go cold, then hot. "Maybe we should stay to help her. This is all my fault."

"Sometimes bad things happen for a reason," Max said. "Perhaps Keeah was meant to do this. I shall stay here. Galen would want me to. But you, you must find the king."

"But —" Eric started.

Julie grabbed Eric's arm. "Keeah has powers. She's got to fight Sparr. And we've got to do this!"

Neal grabbed Eric's other arm. "Let's go!"

As the wolves leaped for Sparr and his

Ninns, the three friends scrambled through the halls.

They shivered as they dashed down the steps.

Their hearts raced as they entered a world of ice.

Eight

Race Against Time

Julie and Eric hitched up reins and saddles on three shaggy pilkas while Neal wrestled open the large city gate.

"Let's find the king!" Eric said firmly, snapping the reins of his pilka.

"Giddyap!" Neal shouted, jumping on his own.

At once, the pilkas took off. They raced past the city gates and out over the crunchy ground. The storm wrapped around them swiftly.

Soon, the palace was out of sight.

"King Zello!" Eric cried.

His voice was lost in the howling wind.

"The storm is getting worse!" said Julie.

"And it's nearly nighttime!" Neal shouted. "Perfect time for this kind of nightmare!"

Still, the six-legged pilkas galloped on. They stormed through an icy forest. Icicles fell like daggers from frozen branches. Tall trees cracked in half, their black limbs heavy with silver ice.

"This place really is cursed," said Julie.

Neal cupped his hands together. "King Zello!" he yelled. "Oh, man, he'll never hear us. He could be miles away. He could even be —"

"Don't say it!" Eric cried, standing in his

saddle. He called out even louder. "Zello! Zello!"

The wind roared like Sparr's deep laughter.

Eric's arms and legs ached. He felt cold. He felt like going to sleep. Frost began to form on all their cheeks. It was getting darker. And colder.

"No!" Eric cried, snapping the reins again. "We have to do this! We have to make it right! Keep yelling, everybody! Keep yelling!"

"King Zello!" they shouted at the top of their lungs. "King Zello!"

Then, they heard it. A faraway sound.

A familiar noise above the wild snowstorm.

Hrrr!

"Hey! I'd recognize that sound anywhere!" Julie shouted. "It's Leep!"

"Yes!" Eric cried. "And where Leep is, there's — King Zello! Zello!"

A dark shape galloped suddenly toward them.

It was Leep. And on the sled behind him, King Zello.

The king pulled up sharply on the reins.

"Galen is frozen!" Eric cried, jumping from his pilka. "And Sparr and Keeah are fighting! There are lots of Ninns, too. A whole army of Ninns!"

"I have an army, too," the king said. He waved his hand behind him.

"Whoa!" Eric exclaimed.

Behind the king, riding on their own sleds, were dozens of men and women. But mostly there were children. Lots and lots of children.

"Wow, an army of Droon kids!" Neal said.

"But how will we fight the big Ninns?" one young girl asked.

Julie jumped down from her saddle. "Hey, I just thought of something. With this curse, we almost forgot the best thing about snow."

Neal frowned. "What's that?"

Julie dug her hands into a high drift and grinned. "The good old Upper World . . . snowball!"

The children of Droon crowded around them.

"We'll help, too," one of them said. "We want to keep our city free."

"And maybe we can use these!" one boy said. From his coat he pulled a Y-shaped stick.

"A slingshot?" said Ned. "Cool! But you have to remember rule number one. When you're fighting Ninns, you pack your snowballs hard!"

The children of Droon dug into the snow eagerly. Soon everyone had made dozens of snowballs. They filled their pockets with them.

"To the palace!" the king called out. At once his sled thundered across the snow.

"Yahoo!" Eric said as he snapped the reins of his pilka. "Sparr and his Ninns will never know what hit them!"

Nine

Droonians, Unite!

The armored red warriors were waiting on the palace steps as the sleds and pilkas roared into the city.

"Come on, everybody!" Eric said, gathering the kids of Droon together. "Snowballs out!"

"Snowballs out!" the kids replied.

"Ready," said Neal. "Aim —"

"And . . . fire!" shouted Julie.

Splat! Splat! Splat!

"Aggkh!" the Ninns cried. Half of them dropped their bows. The other half fell to the steps, clutching their shoulders and knees.

"Yes!" Neal whooped. "Kids one, Ninns zero!"

"To the throne room!" King Zello shouted, rushing past the Ninns and into the palace.

Blam! Crash! Kkkk! Poom!

When they entered the round room, Keeah and Sparr were flinging lightning bolts at each other.

"Whoa!" said Eric. "Keeah is awesome! I guess she figured out the magic!"

A band of angry Ninns rushed at the kids, but the red wolves lunged, forcing the Ninns back.

Then Max swung down from the ceiling and sprayed sticky silk on them.

"Excellent!" Julie shouted. "Come on,

kids, let's finish the job!" She and the children of Droon pelted the tangled Ninns with snowballs.

King Zello led the grown-ups in a charge at Sparr. "Keeah, help Galen!" he boomed.

Keeah rushed to the old wizard, reaching for her velvet pouch.

Fwing! A Ninn arrow whizzed by her side. Keeah looked down. The pouch was slit in half.

The sparkling dust spilled across the floor!

"Oh, no —" she cried.

Blam! Sparr hurled a bolt at Keeah, knocking her roughly into her father. They fell to the floor.

Eric looked around. "I'm going for the amulet!" he cried. "Neal, cover me!"

"You got it!" Neal yelled. "Finally, I get

to try my twisty fastball!" He pelted Sparr with snowballs all the way.

Splat! Splat! Splat! The sorcerer fell back.

Eric took a long slide toward the amulet.

Suddenly — *kkkk-blam!*

A beam of green light shot out from the amulet's crystal. Its light blasted the stone floor.

"Umph!" Eric was thrown backward into Neal. They hit the floor hard. Near them, the giant map of Droon glowed where the beam hit.

Sparr began to laugh wildly. "Yes! Yes! Yes!"

"What, what, what?" Neal snapped.

"The Dust Hills of Panjibarrh!" the sorcerer howled. "That is where great Zor lies sleeping!"

"Sleeping?" said Eric. "But isn't he dead?"

"The giant shall rise again!" Sparr cried. His fins turned black. He pulled his sword out of the floor. Then he towered over Eric and Neal.

"Um . . . any ideas, pal?" Eric mumbled.

Neal shrugged. He dug his hands into his pockets. "Sorry, man. Out of ammo."

"I'm not!" Keeah cried. In a single motion, she twirled to her feet, faced Sparr, and thrust out both of her hands. Before he could move —

KKKK-BLAM! The room went totally white.

"Ahhhhh!" Eric screamed, shutting his eyes.

"Yeeooww!" Neal yelped, covering his face.

But when the light vanished, Sparr was slumped against the wall.

"You!" he shrieked at the princess. "You

have wounded me!" He fell to the floor, yowling in pain like an injured animal.

He clutched the amulet tightly. "All of you will pay for this!"

Ninns surrounded him and pulled him to his feet. Waving their weapons at the kids, they dragged Lord Sparr quickly from the room.

The red wolves howled and chased them to the gates of the city. A moment later, the wolves trotted back.

Sparr was gone.

"Hooray!" the children of Droon cheered. They jumped for joy. "We did it! He's gone!"

Neal rushed over to them. "Slap me five, Droon kids!" he cried. They slapped Neal's hands. Then they did the same to one another.

Suddenly, the throne room went quiet.

Keeah looked up at Galen. She held the

empty velvet bag. "I have failed you again. My magic is gone. I am not worthy of being a wizard."

Everyone stared at the old man's icy face. Max covered his own.

Then the stony silence gave way to another sound.

The sound of wings.

Ten

Reverse the Curse!

The white falcon descended from the frosty air. She hovered above their heads.

"Keeah, my daughter!" the falcon said. "Zello, my king!"

Zello gazed up. "I have missed you!"

"Mother!" the princess said. "Sparr is gone, but his curse remains." She held up the empty velvet bag. "Galen is frozen. My people are frozen! The magic is all gone!"

"Keeah, my time here is almost done,"

the falcon said, fluttering up. "Already I have begun to change. I cannot help you now."

Eric, Julie, and Neal crowded around Keeah.

"How can I cure Galen?" she asked.

The falcon flapped her wings just above the princess. The bird's feathers started to shed. "Remember this always — *you are the magic!* Look into your heart, my child, and you will know."

The bird rose slowly up to the ceiling. Feathers fell away with every flap of her wings. They whirled around like snowflakes in the cold air.

"When next you see me, I shall be in another form. Many trials lie ahead before I can undo this curse. Before I can be your mother again."

"You are my mother always!" Keeah said.

"Soon, I shall see you again!" her

mother called out. "Soon, Keeah! Soon, my brave king!"

A moment later, the falcon was no more than a sparkling blue light vanishing to nothing.

"Wow," Eric whispered.

The last white feather fluttered down slowly. Keeah reached up, clutched it, and held it tight.

Her father whispered to the air above them, "We will find you, my queen. We will help you."

Finally, Keeah looked at the old wizard. "A lightning bolt isn't going to help me now."

Max scuttled over to her. "Queen Relna said if you look into your heart you will know."

"I just thought of something else," said Neal. "I tasted the magic sugar after your mom zapped it. It was good, but pretty regular."

"Yes?" Keeah said.

"Well, I was thinking," Neal said. "What if the magic sugar was just, you know, sugar?"

"It worked when I unfroze the wolves," the princess said.

"But maybe for you, what you touch is magic," said Eric. "Because you are who you are."

Julie nodded. "It's like your mother said: '*You* are the magic.'"

Keeah blinked. "By myself? With no spells?"

"Yes!" the kids said together.

King Zello put his arm around his daughter. "I believe you can do it. I've watched you. You are your mother's daughter."

"Even Sparr said so," Neal added. "And he was scared of you."

Keeah took a deep breath. Then she bent down to the floor. She filled her hand with powdery flakes of snow. She stepped over to Galen and sprinkled the flakes over him.

The flakes danced slowly as they came down.

The ice began to melt from Galen's cheeks. His forehead. His eyes.

The old wizard's face softened. He smiled.

"Keeah!" he said. "I am alive again!"

"Master!" Max said, jumping up and down. "Welcome back to the world of the living!"

Keeah's eyes were wide with amazement. "If it works for you, then . . ." She rushed outside. The city around her lay frozen and white.

"My people! My city!" she called out.

Taking another handful of snow, she tossed it into the air. All at once, the whirling flakes became the soft white petals of apple blossoms!

The clouds swept away. Golden sunlight flooded the square.

Crrrack! Fountains suddenly crackled and spurted with fragrant water. Ice melted from the trees. Their bright green leaves swung loose. The air was full of sweet-scented flowers.

All the ice and snow across the city vanished under the warm sun.

"Spring is back in Jaffa City!" King Zello exclaimed. "Keeah, you have done it!"

Everyone who had been turned to ice began to move again. Soon there was laughter coming from every corner of the vast city.

"Awesome!" Eric said, smiling.

"Now, that's what I call true magic!" Neal said.

The kids shed their spider-silk coats and stood in the bright sunshine.

"This is more like it!" said Julie.

"And look!" Max pointed to the sky over the city's golden walls.

In the bright pink sky above a nearby hill were the rainbow-colored stairs.

The stairs to the Upper World.

The stairs back to Eric's house.

"I guess it's time," said Neal.

"We'd better go," Eric added, "so we can come back again as soon as possible!"

"Thank you for everything!" Galen said. "Once again, you have helped our world."

"And," boomed the king, "I proclaim that the next time you come to Jaffa City, it will be Eric and Julie and Neal Day!"

"It's a deal!" said Neal.

Everyone cheered. The crowd followed the three Upper Worlders to the foot of the magic stairway.

"Good-bye, for now," Keeah said, hugging her friends. "And come back soon!"

"That's a deal, too!" Eric said.

The three friends ran up the stairs. They entered the small room at the top.

Neal clicked the light switch. The room lit up.

Whoosh! The stairs vanished and the basement floor appeared beneath them.

The world of Droon was secret once more.

"What do you think Sparr's going to do with that amulet?" Neal asked when they slipped quietly out of the small room.

"I think we'll find out real soon," Julie said.

Sunlight streamed through the basement windows. The clock told them no time had passed.

Eric picked up the softball and tossed it. "Even though today was dangerous, I have to admit, it was pretty cool."

"Correction," said Neal, grabbing the ball and tossing it himself. "Cold, very cold."

"The word I would use is *icy*," Julie said. Then she stole the ball from Neal and ran up the stairs. "Last one in the backyard is a rotten egg!"

Eric and Neal shot looks at each other.

"Me first!" they both cried as they dashed up the stairs after her.

The Sleeping
Giant of Goll

To Robert Boyd
and Amanda Barrett,
who know that plain old life
is an adventure

Contents

One

The Magic Staircase

Bing-bing-bing!

It was early Saturday morning.

Eric Hinkle bounced up from his bed and shut off the alarm. He stared into the dim light, trying to recall his dream. Then he remembered it.

"Oh, no," he groaned. "Another night without dreaming of Droon!"

Dreaming was important.

After Eric and his friends visited Droon,

Princess Keeah told them that their dreams would tell them when to return. But it had been two weeks since anyone had dreamed of Droon.

That meant something was wrong.

Very wrong.

"The magic has to keep working," Eric said to himself. "It just has to!"

He dressed quickly and snuck down to the kitchen. He tiptoed to the back door and unlocked it. His best friend, Neal Kroger, slid in quietly.

"What's to eat?" Neal asked.

Eric stared at him. "Never mind food," he said. "What did you dream about last night?"

Neal took a deep breath. "The usual. Pizza."

Eric moaned. "Pizza? No wonder you're hungry."

"In my dream I was sitting in the middle of a humongous pizza," Neal said. "And I had to eat my way out to the crust. What about you?"

Eric sighed. "I was hitting a metal garbage can with a broomstick. Bing, bang, bong all night."

"Did it wake your parents?" Neal asked.

Eric gave him a look. "No. Then I woke up and realized it was just my alarm going off."

Neal shook his head as they tramped down the stairs to the basement. "Doesn't sound like we'll be going to Droon today," he said.

"I can't believe this," Eric groaned.

He remembered the first time he, Neal, and Julie discovered the magic entrance to Droon.

They were cleaning up Eric's messy basement when they found a small closet hidden under the stairs.

They went inside, flicked off the light, and — *whoosh!* — the floor turned into a rainbow-colored staircase.

Of course they went down the stairs.

Soon, they met Princess Keeah and the wizard Galen. They helped them fight a wicked and very powerful sorcerer named Lord Sparr. They had gone on lots of adventures since then.

Until now.

"What about the soccer ball?" Neal asked.

Princess Keeah had put a spell on their soccer ball. It would float in the air and become a globe of Droon when she needed them most.

Eric shook his head. "It's busted. Look."

He picked up the ball from its place on

the workbench. He dropped the ball to the floor.

Boing! It bounced back.

"This ball is only good for playing soccer."

Neal twisted his face into a frown. "Keeah said we'd return to Droon as long as the magic keeps working. I guess we're not going back."

"Oh, man!" Eric whined. "Julie will be sad."

"Or mad," Neal said. "We'd better tell her."

"Tell me what?" Julie said as she ran down the stairs. "Your mom said it was okay to come down, Eric. Am I too early?"

"More like too late," Eric said, shooting a look at Neal. "You didn't happen to have a dream about Droon last night, did you?"

Julie shook her head. "No . . ."

"That's it," Neal said. "Good-bye, Droon."

Julie grinned. "I mean, no, it wasn't just *any* dream. . . ." She headed straight for the door under the stairs.

"What?" Eric turned to her. "You mean —"

Julie laughed. "Last night I had the *ultimate* dream about Droon! I was floating high over the countryside. Then I saw a bunch of crowns — gold crowns — just sitting on a hilltop in the middle of nowhere!"

"Cool!" Neal exclaimed.

"But," Julie continued, "the coolest part was that I had a crown, too. I was Princess Julie! It was so awesome. We are definitely going back. Now!"

"Yes — yes — yes!" Eric yelled. "Let's do it!"

Julie quickly pulled open the small door. She waved her hand in. "Enter."

They all piled in. Neal closed the door.

Julie flicked off the light.

Click! It was dark for an instant. Then —

Whoosh! The floor vanished beneath them. In its place was the top step of the magical rainbow-colored staircase. The staircase to Droon.

Eric jumped. "It's so good to be going back!"

"What can I say?" Julie said. "I'm special."

"You better believe it!" Neal said. "We'd actually have to finish cleaning Eric's basement if it wasn't for you!"

The three friends climbed down the rainbow steps. Cool air wafted up from below. It smelled sweet. The sky was pink and purple with streaks of bright orange. The sun was just about to rise.

"It's nearly dawn here," said Neal. "Hey, look at those trees."

The stairs ended in a misty grove of low, blossoming trees overlooking a clear green lake. The pink morning mist clung to the branches.

The kids jumped off the staircase just as the steps faded from sight. Eric knew the stairs would reappear when it was time to leave.

"I am so glad to be here," he said.

Julie looked around. "This is weird. Nine trees in a perfect circle. Trees don't normally grow in a circle. I think someone planted them this way."

"Maybe there are people nearby," Eric added.

Suddenly, the branches twitched.

"Did you see that?" Neal asked.

Before Eric could answer, the trees leaned their trunks toward the children.

Their rough branches thrust down like arms, grabbed Julie, and tightly curled their waxy leaves around her like fingers.

Then one of the trees pulled her off the ground.

"Helpppp!" she cried, struggling to get free.

But Eric and Neal couldn't help her.

One tree seized Neal by the ankles and pulled him up sharply. Another clutched Eric's waist and dragged him off his feet.

"Let us go, you overgrown twigs!" Eric shouted, smacking at the branches to get free.

But the trees only tightened their grip.

Two

The Land of Living Trees

"Now I know what they mean by plant food," Neal groaned as the tree holding him swung around. "And I think we're it!"

Julie's tree shook her up and down. "I promise I'll never eat a vegetable again. Just let us go!"

But the trees didn't let go.

They swung the kids high over the ground.

"Oo-oo-oo-oh!" Eric moaned. "I feel si-i-ick!"

The branches only coiled more tightly around him. He felt his strength slipping away.

"This can't happen!" he cried, gasping for breath.

"This is Droo-oo-oon," Neal cried. "Anything can happen!"

"I wish Keeah and Galen were here," Julie yelped. "They'd make these trees act like trees!"

At that moment, the sun began to rise.

Golden light slanted across the tree-tops.

Suddenly, the trees lowered their branches. They loosened their grip, and the children slid to the ground.

The trees coiled back to their original shapes.

And went completely still.

It was a quiet circle of trees once more.

Eric scrambled over to his friends. "Are you guys okay?" he asked.

"Ask me later," Neal coughed. "For now, let's just get out of here."

"I agree," Julie said, rubbing her arms where the branches had clutched her. "That sure was a Droonian moment."

Eric pointed to the lake at the bottom of the hill. "Let's get down there. Fast!"

They hurried to the sandy shore. The lake water glistened like glass. A light breeze rose off the surface.

"Peaceful," Julie said. "I wonder where —"

Splish! Splorsh!

The center of the lake began to bubble. Neal stepped back. "Okay, now what?"

The water splashed. A small round eye pierced the surface. Then a long curved neck.

"Now — we hide!" Eric said, pulling Neal and Julie facedown in the sand.

"Sppp — ah!" Neal spit out sand as he looked across the water. "Terrific. Weird eyeball, long neck. This means only one thing. Sea serpent!"

"It's a lake," said Julie.

"Lake serpent!" Neal cried.

Soon, a body rose from the water. It was green and short and stubby, about the size of a small car. Sunlight flashed off its wet side.

"That's not a serpent," Julie said. "It's a . . ."

Vrrrm! It rumbled up onto the beach on fat green wheels. It lurched to a halt in the sand.

"A lake serpent with *wheels*?" Eric said.

Boing! A hatch on the side popped open.

A head appeared. Then a face. The head had bright orange hair that stood

straight up. In the middle of the face was a little pug nose.

"Max!" Julie exclaimed, jumping up and running over to the green machine.

Eric nudged Neal. "You were so afraid. Can't you tell the difference between a serpent and a submarine?"

"Afraid?" Neal shrugged. "I call it being *careful*."

Max clambered down from the hatch. He saluted with three of his eight legs. "Your favorite spider troll — at your service!"

He tapped the side of the sub. *Boink! Boink!*

Two more heads appeared from the hatch.

One was a young girl with long blonde hair. She was wearing a jeweled crown. The other was an old man with a long white beard and frizzy hair.

"Princess Keeah! And Galen!" Eric said. "Boy, are we glad to see you guys!"

"As we are to see you," Princess Keeah said. "You've come just in time to help us again."

"But we almost didn't make it," Neal said. "Some trees attacked us!"

"Then the sun rose and they let us go," Eric added.

"But mostly, I had the greatest dream," Julie said. "I even had a crown!" Then she told them all about it.

"Time will tell what it all means," Keeah said.

Galen smiled. "And what do you think of my latest invention? I call it my Below-Water-Motor-Powered-Transportation Vehicle."

Neal frowned. "You mean . . . a sub?"

"Sub?" Galen looked quizzically at

Neal. "I like that name. Sub. It certainly saves time."

"Which is good," Max chirped. "Because our time is running out. We're on a mission to find Lord Sparr!"

"Come aboard," Galen told the children. "I will explain."

A moment later, the three friends joined Keeah, Max, and Galen inside the small ship.

"Very cool!" Eric said as they took seats in a small round cabin. A control panel circled the front wall under a large window.

Max took hold of the controls. He pushed a large green button. Motors whirred behind them. The small ship rumbled down the beach to the water.

"We're on our way to Panjibarrh," Keeah said. "It's where the terrible giant, Zor, is supposed to have been buried. Lord Sparr is there."

"Dive, Max!" Galen commanded. "Dive!"

As the submarine splashed down into the green lake, Eric turned to his friends. "I think this is one adventure we'll always remember."

"For starters, we've never been attacked by trees before," Julie whispered.

"And I've never been in a sub before," said Neal. "Blub-blub!"

Three

Mirror, Mirror, in the Sub

The underwater world was beautiful.

Thick bunches of sea vines coiled up from below. Bright red balloon plants puffed and unpuffed as they passed.

A school of yellow lumpy fish swam by, grinning right into the window.

"This is awesome," Eric said.

"I'm sure glad we're in here," Neal added.

Keeah smiled. "It won't be long now. Lord Sparr is nearby. We are getting close."

Galen pointed to a map on the control panel next to Max. "We have tracked Sparr to the Dust Hills of Panjibarrh. Legend says that is where the giant, Zor, lies buried in his lost tomb."

Eric shuddered as he remembered their last adventure. The evil sorcerer Sparr stole an ancient piece of jewelry. It was called the amulet of Zor.

The amulet was supposed to have the power to bring the giant back to life.

Max twittered nervously. "They say when the giant lived, he was taller than a mountain!"

"With luck, we'll stop the big guy," Neal said.

"With luck and with help," Keeah said,

touching a single white feather that hung on a silver chain around her neck.

The kids knew what it was.

It was a feather from Keeah's mother, Queen Relna. A spell had transformed her into a white falcon. But she had changed shape again.

No one knew what shape the queen had now.

The princess smiled, touching the feather again. "This makes me feel as if she is with me."

Zzzzt!

"What's that sound? Are we leaking?" Neal said, whirling on his seat. "Because I don't like leaks when I'm in a sub."

"It is Galen's magic mirror," said Max. "It has something for us to see. . . ."

The wizard stepped over to an old mirror hanging on the back wall of the sub.

The mirror allowed the wizard to see what was happening in different parts of Droon. The rippling surface flickered with a dull glow.

The kids already knew what was about to happen. They had seen the mirror before in Galen's tower.

Galen waved his hand and the mirror cleared.

"There's a dark room," Keeah said, peering at the image. "It's dusty and dirty and very large. Big stones are everywhere."

"It is a tomb," Galen said softly. "And look!"

Stomping toward the mirror was the sorcerer himself. Lord Sparr.

His long black cloak swept across the floor of the tomb. And the pointed purple fins behind his ears certainly didn't make him look any friendlier.

"I see we're tuned to the wicked sorcerer station," Neal said. "Man, he gives me the creeps."

Surrounding Sparr was a troop of plump, red-faced warriors in black armor. They carried shovels and picks and torches.

"Here!" the sorcerer said, pointing down.

Flickering torchlight glowed on a large, dusty stone. A strange symbol was carved on it.

"The sign of Zor!" Keeah gasped. "Sparr has already found the lost tomb!"

Sparr's eyes flashed. He shivered as he stood over the large stone. "So . . . I have found the lost empire. And the legend is true. Zor lies here."

"Lost empire?" Eric whispered.

Galen sighed deeply. "Droon is a world with a long past, my friends. Lord Sparr has discovered what remains of the ancient dark realm of Goll. It is an empire whose cities now lie buried beneath the earth but that once ruled this world. Goll is a lost civilization. An empire that time forgot."

"Too bad Sparr remembered," said Neal.

The sorcerer snapped his fingers, and his Ninn warriors began quickly digging around the edges of the stone.

Clank! Clong! Before long, the Ninns pulled the stone from the floor. They looked down. They backed away from the hole, trembling.

"Have you found . . . him?" Sparr said.

The Ninns muttered to themselves.

Sparr pushed them out of the way and leaned over the hole. His fins turned pale, almost white.

The mirror zoomed in. There, lying open to the flickering torchlight, was a large dark object.

"Oh, my!" Max muttered.

"What is it?" Eric asked.

"It's a . . . a . . . head!" Keeah gasped.

The head was six feet long from chin to brow. The large eyes were closed. The dust of centuries covered the cheeks and lips.

But the strangest part was the skin.

It was dark and smooth and glimmered golden red in the torchlight.

"He's . . . made of metal!" Eric said.

"Bronze," Galen muttered. "Zor is a giant made of bronze. He walked the earth long ago."

Neal stared at the mirror. "A giant, huh? If that's just his head, this guy must be huge!"

"Bigger than huge," said Eric. "Enormous."

"Enormous? Ha!" said Neal. "He's hu-mongous! He's colossal! He's —"

"Will you shhh!" Julie hissed.

"We are afraid, Lord Sparr," one of the Ninns whispered. "We want to go home."

"Home!" Sparr snarled. "My true home lies above, in the Upper World! The only way for me to get home is with this giant's help!"

Eric stopped breathing. *Home? In the Upper World? In my world?*

"What does that mean?" Neal asked.

Julie started trembling. "He's scaring me."

"Dig, my Ninns! Dig!" Sparr shouted. "Dig up the rest of him! Zor shall rise again!"

As the Ninns dug away at the huge stones, the sorcerer stormed away into the tomb's darkness.

Zzzzt. The mirror faded.

The front window of the sub bubbled furiously. The water seemed lighter. Max was steering the ship up through the water.

Up to the surface.

Galen nodded gravely. "Now our real journey begins. Our journey to find Lord Sparr. And to stop him!"

Julie peered through the window as the sub splashed above the surface. "There's land ahead. A long beach and big brown hills beyond."

Keeah nodded. "The shores of Panjibarrh. They call it the land of dust."

Neal gulped loudly. "Just so everybody knows," he said, "I'm allergic to dust."

Four

Welcome to Panjibarrh!

The submarine rumbled out onto the beach and stopped on the sand.

Pop! Everyone piled out of the top hatch.

Before them stretched a row of small hills. Behind that was a range of larger hills. Beyond that were even taller hills. As far as the eye could see, everything was dusty, brown, and smooth.

"Panjibarrh seems kind of boring," Neal said.

"Let us hope it stays boring," Max chirped. "But this is Droon. Anything can happen."

Galen turned to the ship, uttered a short command, and the ship rumbled back into the water.

Keeah scanned the hills. Then she took a deep breath and clutched her feather necklace.

"Lord Sparr is somewhere in these hills," she said. "I can feel him nearby. Let's find him."

For the next hour, the small band climbed through narrow passes that ran between the hillsides. From one range to another, the six travelers slowly wormed their way upward.

Entering one steep pass, Galen stopped.

He turned his head slowly. He narrowed his eyes.

"There . . ." he murmured. "That shadowy hole in the rocks. There is something in there."

Max began to quake. "What is it, master?"

Galen gazed deeply into the shadows. "A cave. And — *he* is there." He turned to Keeah.

"Princess," he said, "I sense something evil in there. If what I feel in my heart is true, Sparr's plan is even more terrible than we thought. I must go in. You and the others wait here."

"Be careful, master," Max chittered.

The wizard smiled at the spider troll. "My time has not yet come, my friend. Don't worry."

With that, Galen wrapped his robe around him and entered the cave alone.

Strange sounds echoed suddenly from the hills above. Low, rumbling sounds. Then the air went still. Silence fell over the pass.

"That's weird," Julie whispered. "It's like all the sound in the world just stopped."

Neal squinted up at the hills. "Do you think it's Lord Sparr —"

Whoosh!

A burst of wind swept up from the dusty ground. It spun faster and faster. It coiled around in the air, forming a dark, whirling funnel.

"Yikes!" said Eric, shielding his eyes. "Let's get out of here!"

But the wind struck quickly. As if it were alive, the coil of spinning dust leaped upon the five friends, scattering them.

"Take cover, everyone!" Keeah cried out, grabbing Max and pulling him to the shelter of an overhanging rock.

Julie tried to join them but stumbled on the rocky ground. She struggled to her feet, but the funnel tore after her, whirling and spitting dust.

"Help!" she cried, trying to outrun the wind.

Neal bolted from his hiding place. "Julie!"

Keeah, too, leaped from shelter to face the furious funnel. She clutched her feather and cried out, but her words were lost in the fury of the storm.

The wind swept around Julie, surrounding her. "It's got me!" she shrieked.

The wind pulled her inside itself.

Eric stumbled toward the funnel, his arms outstretched. "Julie! Here!" he shouted. The spinning dust stung his face. "I'm coming!" he cried.

But the wind wouldn't let him come.

The twister spun Julie around and

around. It roared up the side of the pass. Up and up it went, spinning Julie away with it, until her cries were lost.

"JULIE!" Eric shouted for the last time.

A moment later, the dark funnel was gone.

The wind in the pass died down to nothing.

The storm was over.

And Julie was gone.

Five

A Hidden Village

"The storm went that way!" Keeah said, pointing to the highest range of hills. "We have to find Julie. And we need to hurry. Come on!"

"What about Galen?" Neal asked.

"He is Droon's greatest wizard," said Max, already scampering up the hillside after Keeah. "Galen Longbeard can take care of himself!"

The four friends raced into the hills, following the track of the dust storm. Hill after hill they climbed. Higher and higher they went.

"What if we can't find her?" said Neal, breathing hard as he scrambled up a rocky hillside.

"No way!" Eric snapped. "Julie's special. We'll find her. We've got to keep going. We've got to."

Max spun a spider silk rope and swung from ledge to ledge, moving ahead of everyone.

Suddenly, he stopped and pointed his pug nose in the air. He sniffed. "Smoke," he said.

"Smoke usually means people," said Keeah.

Neal nodded. "Be careful. Careful is good."

They followed the smoky smell until they came to a break between the hills.

Clustered along one hillside were dozens of small houses. They had domed roofs made of dried mud.

Smoke wafted up from their chimneys.

"A village," Eric whispered.

In the exact center of the village was a large round platform.

It looked like a giant wheel lying on its side.

And in the exact center of the wheel was —

"Julie!" Keeah said.

Surrounding Julie were hundreds of small creatures covered in red fur. Each one was about three feet tall. They had doglike snouts covered with whiskers, except for small black noses at the tips. Their ears were pointy and very long.

"She's a prisoner," Neal said. "And we're outnumbered. Any ideas?"

"Perhaps a little magic will help," Keeah

said. She waved her hand over the four of them. The air turned a misty pink.

"The fog of invisibility!" Max chirped. "Galen taught you well, Princess. Come, let us enter."

Hidden by the pink fog, the four friends crept quietly into the village. No one saw them.

The largest of the strange, furry creatures stepped across the giant wheel to Julie.

"Now . . ." he said, curling and uncurling his nose whiskers, ". . . now, you will get it!"

Julie shook her head. "No . . . please . . ."

Eric stole a look at Neal and Keeah. "She's in trouble. We need to get her out of there — now!"

"Bring the black helmet!" the furry creature commanded. "I, Batamogi, King of the Oobja, shall put it right on her head!"

Eric couldn't stand it anymore. He jumped out of the pink fog and ran up to the platform.

"Stop!" he shouted at the top of his lungs. "Julie is our friend. You leave her alone!"

All the pointy-eared creatures turned.

Julie blinked over their heads. "Eric?"

The small, furry king turned. "Who is *Eric*?"

"*I'm* Eric!" said Eric. "And if you hurt Julie, we'll be all over you like . . . like . . ."

Neal jumped out of the fog next to Eric. "Like cheese on a pizza!"

"So don't hurt her!" Keeah shouted, jumping out of the fog with Max.

Batamogi stumbled backward. "*Hurt* her? But . . . Julie is our new princess! She has come to help our people. We are going to *crown* her."

Eric frowned. "What? Oh, sure. Crown her. With something nasty called the *black helmet?*"

The fox-eared leader held up the shiny helmet.

It was covered with beautiful jewels.

"Black goes better with her hair," the king said. "We have a nice pink helmet and two powder-blue ones. But I think black is her color."

Eric blinked. "Oh . . . um . . . well . . ."

Julie laughed and jumped over to her friends. "These people aren't hurting me," she said. "The storm set me down in their village. They've been really, really nice! And it's just like my dream!"

She turned to the crowd. "Everybody, meet Eric, Neal, Keeah, and Max."

The furry king bowed nearly to the ground. "I am Batamogi, King of the Oobja. We are the mole people of the Panjibarrh hills."

Batamogi bowed again to Keeah. "Welcome, Princess. All of Droon knows you. But there is another princess here, too. Princess Julie."

He handed Julie the shiny black helmet encrusted with jewels.

Julie laughed. "I'm really just a regular kid."

The king tapped his furry head. "All mole people can sense things. We can tell when someone has powers even before they do. And believe me, Julie, you have powers. You will help us, you'll see."

Julie blinked as she slid the jeweled helmet on. "Cool," she said. "But I still don't believe it."

Keeah turned to the fox-eared, red-furred king. "We have come here to find Lord Sparr."

The mole people gasped and pulled back.

"Sparr!" Batamogi snorted with anger. "We do not like him. We are peaceful people. But Sparr demanded we show him where Zor's tomb is. We have known for ages that Zor lies in the ancient realm of Goll. It is right under these hills. When my brothers refused to tell Sparr, he took them away. He said that he would hurt them if I didn't show him where the giant was buried."

Batamogi sniffled and wiped his snout on his furry wrist. "I had to do what he asked!"

"That's why we're here," Eric said. "We need to stop Sparr from bringing Zor back to life."

The Oobja king sniffled once more, then stood up straight. "Then I will show you where Sparr and his Ninns are. Yes! But first, we feast. Come, my people. Click-clack!"

The Oobja people laughed softly to themselves and scurried away on their short legs. Moments later they were back, carrying a flat, round bread as big as the big wooden wheel itself.

"Flat bread baked with red sauce and cheese," Batamogi said. "We like them big. Sometimes we sit in the middle and eat our way to the crust!"

Neal's mouth dropped open. He stared at Eric. "Whoa! I guess I *did* dream of Droon last night. Only I didn't know it."

Eric smiled as he chewed. He wondered if he, too, had dreamed of Droon without knowing it.

"Eat up!" Batamogi urged. "Our mission is dangerous."

He ripped off a piece of cheesy bread and, bowing his head, handed it to Princess Julie.

"And Lord Sparr will do everything he can to stop us!"

Six

A New Enemy?

Batamogi led the children down from the big round platform. His people joined him.

"What is the big wheel, anyway?" Eric asked.

The Oobja king smoothed his whiskers. "Ah, yes, well, let me explain —"

"There's a big stick here," Neal said, peering around the wheel. "Like a control stick. What happens if you push it —"

Errrch! The stick squeaked as Neal touched it.

At once the wheel began to spin. Then a loud whooshing sound came from nowhere. A whirling storm of dust exploded up from the ground. It encircled Neal and swept him up in the air.

"Whoa!" he yelled. "Help me!"

Batamogi quickly pushed the stick back down.

The dust storm disappeared and — *plop!* — Neal landed in a heap on the ground.

Julie laughed. "That's how I got here!"

Batamogi helped Neal up and brushed him off. "We call this our Wind Wheel. We use it to make dust storms to keep others from finding our village. Too bad it didn't keep Sparr from stealing my brothers."

Then the king led the children to the

edge of the village. He turned and waved to his people.

They waved back from the big wheel.

"Where are your brothers?" Keeah asked.

The king tapped his forehead again. "I don't know. But something tells me they are alive."

Sunlight slanted across the dust hills as Batamogi led the troop into a narrow pass. The hills on either side rose hundreds of feet in the air.

The fox-eared king pointed up ahead. "Sparr brought his Ninns through this pass. They came to dig up the giant. We are not far now."

Eric shared a glance with his friends. They were heading straight for Lord Sparr.

"I know I say 'careful' a lot," Neal said. "But maybe now is a good time. You never know when something might —"

Fwap! Fwap! The sound of wings filled the air.

"Hrooooo!" came a loud cry.

"Groggles?" Neal yelped.

"No! Worse!" Batamogi replied. "Hide!"

The air grew hot, and a burst of blue flame shot across the hills above them. Then a giant blue wing flapped overhead. It was scaly and rough. A spiky arm clawed at the sky.

"A dragon!" Keeah whispered, touching her feather necklace. "It's all blue!"

Dust and rocks crumbled from the hillsides and into the pass in front of the kids. The shadow of the dragon's wing glided over them.

"Hrooooo!" The dragon's call coiled down once more. Then the shadow vanished.

Sunlight flooded the high walls again. The dragon was gone.

Batamogi waddled to the middle of the pass and looked up. "This dragon has been here since Sparr arrived, frightening my people. The hills used to be quiet. I hope they will be quiet again."

Clank! Clong! From nearby came the sounds of metal and stone banging together.

"Digging?" Eric whispered.

The king nodded. "Come, we're nearly there."

Quietly, they tiptoed to the end of the passage. Beyond the last range of hills lay a small valley.

"Holy cow!" Julie said.

The valley lay torn open. Piles of sand-colored rocks were strewn about. Flying lizards called groggles whined loudly as they helped to pull large stones out of the ground.

Lord Sparr stood by while hundreds of

his red warrior Ninns dug away at the earth.

"They're digging up the whole tomb," Keeah said. "They've dug up the resting place of Zor."

"He won't be resting long," Max said. "Look!"

Two Ninns dragged a heavy box across the dirt. Eric and his friends recognized that box. It contained Zor's amulet. Sparr had stolen it when he turned Jaffa City to ice. With the amulet, Sparr could bring the dead giant back to life.

The Ninns opened the box. Sparr took out the large black amulet. The jewel in its center glistened in the sunlight. The sorcerer began to laugh.

"He's going to do it!" Neal whispered.

Sparr stepped down into the open tomb. Slowly, he strode across the giant's dark chest.

He set the amulet into a spot near Zor's neck.

Click! It fit perfectly into place.

The air grew hushed in the valley.

"Now what?" Eric whispered.

They heard a grunting noise behind them.

"Uh-oh," Neal mumbled.

The group turned around to find a fat, red-faced Ninn warrior standing over them.

"I've been expecting you!" he growled.

Seven

The Powers of Sparr

"That's it, we're doomed for sure!" Max chittered, scurrying behind his friends.

Then the Ninn smiled. And his fat red face began to change. It went pale, and a long white beard grew from his chin. His warrior's armor shriveled away and became a long blue robe.

"Galen!" Keeah said. "How did you get here?"

The wizard motioned them into the

shadows as he spoke. "The cave I saw was an old entrance to Goll. To avoid being captured, I pretended to be a Ninn. My friends, it's worse than we thought. Sparr wants to raise Zor for one reason only."

Keeah trembled. "What reason?"

"Ages ago, Zor came under the power of something called the Golden Wasp," Galen said. "Only the giant knows where it lies hidden."

"The Golden Wasp!" the princess exclaimed. "One of Sparr's Three Powers!"

Eric, Neal, and Julie shared a look.

They all remembered the first time Galen told them about Sparr's Three Powers. They were magical objects the sorcerer created so that he could take over Droon. When Galen found out, he put a spell over them to change their shape.

Now they were hidden; no one knew where.

The First Power was a jewel called the Red Eye of Dawn. It controlled the forces of nature.

"What does this Wasp thing do?" Neal asked.

"The Wasp is even more dangerous than the Eye of Dawn," Galen told them. "It controls the minds and thoughts of others."

Neal snorted. "Ha! It won't control *my* mind."

"Right," said Eric. "Only pizza does that. And ice cream. And peanut butter. Also nachos."

Neal frowned. "You're making me hungry."

Julie turned to Galen. "What can we do?"

But the wizard didn't answer. His eyes were filled with fear. "Look now!" he said.

Sparr stood over the giant's body. "By

the stars of Droon, rise, O ancient Zor! Rise!"

The ground began to rumble and quake.

Then, all at once, the giant's huge arms burst up from the ground, sending rocks flying everywhere. His legs kicked suddenly, shattering the earth. Then Zor lifted himself out of his tomb.

He struggled to his feet.

His tremendous shadow fell over the valley.

"Uh-oh," said Julie. "We have a problem."

"A big problem," Max chirped.

The dark eyes of the giant stared at the sorcerer beneath him. A simple lift of his foot would crush Lord Sparr in an instant.

But Zor did not crush him. He knelt before Sparr and bowed his head to him.

"Master!" the giant boomed. "What would you have me do?"

"Holy cow!" Eric whispered. "How are we going to stop that thing?"

"We can't!" Max chittered. "We're doomed!"

Sparr's face twisted into an evil grin. "Zor, I command you to find the Golden Wasp!"

Zor turned his head and stared at the sun. His dark eyes took on a fiery glow.

"With the Wasp, I, Lord Sparr, shall conquer all of Droon!" the sorcerer shouted. "Then I shall rise to the Upper World and conquer it, too!"

The Upper World! Eric thought. *My world.*

Sparr thrust his hand into the air. "Go, my giant! Find the Wasp!"

The giant swiveled his enormous body.

Thoom! He took a step.

Thoom! Another step.

"Go!" Sparr cried out. "Let nothing stop you!"

Eric couldn't take any more. He jumped out of the shadows and shook his fist at Zor.

"Nothing but us!" he cried. "We'll stop you!"

Thooom . . . The giant stopped. He turned his enormous bronze face.

He lowered his eyes at Eric and his friends.

"Um," Eric mumbled. "Did I really say that?"

"I think you did," Neal answered.

Sparr whirled around and pointed toward the children. "Zor! Destroy them!"

"Watch out, here he comes!" Batamogi yelled.

An enormous foot slammed to earth near the kids. *Thoom!*

Sparr began to laugh wildly. "Yes! Yes! Destroy them, once and for all!"

The giant's other foot lifted up over the kids.

Its huge shadow fell over them.

"Run!" cried Batamogi at the top of his lungs.

Eight

The Bronze Giant

Keeah leaped over and pushed Eric out of the way just in time.

Thoom! Zor's other foot slammed down. Then he stretched his giant arms toward Keeah.

"No!" Keeah slid down the hill toward Zor.

Suddenly, another cry filled the air. It echoed down from the hills above. "Hrooooo!"

"The blue dragon!" Neal shouted.

The dragon swooped toward Zor, but the giant was swift. He pulled a huge ledge off the side of the hill, broke it in half, and heaved the chunks of rock at the dragon.

"Begone, you beast!" Zor boomed.

The dragon clawed at him, crying out noisily. "Hrooooo — ooo!" Then it swooped down and clamped its jaws tightly on the giant's shoulder.

"ARRGH!" Zor howled, flailing his arms and losing his balance.

Wham! He fell back against the hills, sending a pile of rocks crashing into the valley below.

Eric leaped out of the way, tumbling to the ground next to Neal.

"Did you say something about Panjibarrh being boring?" Eric asked.

"Not me!" Neal said, scrambling away

just before Zor's huge foot slammed down near him.

Sparr's laughter turned to shouting. "Galen, you have bothered me once too often. Prepare to meet your doom!"

His fingertips sizzled with red flame.

The wizard scoffed. "You haven't seen the last of me, Sparr." He sent a bolt of blue light shooting across the valley at the sorcerer.

Ka-boom! It exploded at Sparr's feet, knocking him into the dust.

"It's two against one, Sparr!" Keeah cried. She followed the wizard's bolt with one of her own.

Ka-boom-oom! Sparr fell once again.

Together, the two wizards pushed Sparr deep into the remains of Zor's dark tomb. They followed him down into it, their blue light flashing up from the depths.

The dragon kept up its fierce attack on Zor.

"Arrgh!" the giant bellowed. He swatted the dragon. When it pulled back, he tried to stomp Neal and Julie, but they scurried out of the way.

"Can't catch us!" Julie yelled. "We're special!"

"Hrooooo!" The dragon circled the giant. It opened its jaws wide and breathed a blast of fiery blue flame. Zor shielded his face and stomped away from the children.

Another blast of blue fire sent Zor reeling back even farther.

"The dragon is winning!" Eric shouted.

Then the sky above the valley burned red.

Sparr flew up from the depths of the tomb to a high rock. He shot bolt after bolt of red light back down into the tomb.

And from the tomb's darkness came a scream.

"It's Keeah!" Max cried. "She's in trouble!"

The dragon turned in midflight. Its deep green eyes pierced the dusty air. "Hrooooo!"

Eric stared at the large blue beast. Its eyes showed — what? Fear. And something else, too.

"The dragon needs to help Keeah!" Eric called out. "Come on, guys. Let's keep Zor busy!"

Neal and Julie heaved rocks at the giant. Eric grabbed a Ninn shovel and began whacking Zor's huge feet. *Bing! Bang! Bong!*

"Hey!" Neal shouted. "Your dream, Eric. Hitting a garbage can. That's just what Zor is!"

Eric laughed as he kept on banging. "I *did* dream of Droon after all! Hey, I'm special, too!"

While the dragon flew at Sparr, the sorcerer began uttering strange ancient words.

"*Zor — katoo — selam — teeka — meth!*"

A red cloud swirled up from Sparr and shot across to Zor. The cloud was sucked into the amulet. The amulet's crystal glowed red-hot.

"RRRR!" the giant roared. "Destroy the village! Destroy the village!"

Zor heaved his arms high in the air. He turned to the dust hills and began to climb.

"No!" Batamogi cried. "Oh, my poor people!"

Thomp! Thomp! The earth quaked with each step. A thick cloud of dust poured over the kids.

Eric shielded his eyes, but the dust

stung him. "I can't see anything," he said, stumbling.

Julie rushed to him. "Rub your eyes, Eric."

He balled up his fists and rubbed his eyes to clear them. "Thanks. Now let's get out of here."

Julie stared at Eric. She gasped. She whirled to her feet. "That's it! Come on, everybody! We can stop this nasty metal-brained giant."

"How?" Neal asked, running after her.

"With what these hills are famous for," said Julie. "Dust!"

Nine

Dust Is Our Friend

Thomp! Thomp! The giant clomped up the hills toward the Oobja village.

Batamogi waddled as fast as his short legs could carry him. His whiskers curled in fear. "I hope we can save my people!"

Julie raced next to him, her black helmet shining in the afternoon sun. "We'll save them. Don't worry."

Wham! Bam! Zor hurled boulders at the kids.

"Well, okay. Worry a little!" Julie said, pulling the king out of the way just as a boulder crashed nearby.

They dashed through the pass and into the village before Zor got there.

The Oobja were hiding in their homes.

The kids rushed to the big wooden wheel.

Batamogi ran to the control stick. "Princess Julie, the honor is yours!"

Julie nodded, then pulled the control stick as Neal had done before. *Errrch!* The Wind Wheel began to turn. It spun faster and faster.

Whooosh! A dark funnel of dust started up from the middle of the wheel. It rose high into the sky, spinning like a tornado.

"I'm good at controlling things," Max chirped. "Let me help." He wrapped his eight legs around the control stick and pulled hard.

King Batamogi joined him.

Whooosh! The dust funnel shot up the hillside.

Then, there he was.

Zor. His giant bronze head peered between two peaks. He hoisted himself up and climbed through. "ARRR!" he bellowed down at them.

Just as he lifted his giant foot to stomp the village, the dust storm spun up at him.

Zor raised his giant arms in front of his face. He backed away, pawing at the spinning wind.

"He can't see," Eric said. "It's working!"

Zor backed up to the summit of the highest hill. He shielded his eyes with one hand and swatted the brown spinning air with the other.

Still the dust storm came at him.

Zor stepped backward once more.

Krrrakk! The ledge beneath him gave way.

"AHHH!" the giant screamed.

He tumbled backward off the mountain and hit the valley below with a thundering crash. *BOO-OOM!*

Batamogi and Max slowed the wheel. The dust storm died away. The village fell quiet.

The kids rushed down to the giant metal man. His bronze body was cracked and crumpled.

He shuddered, then lay still.

His giant lips quivered.

"Shh, everyone," Eric said, creeping slowly closer. "Zor's going to say something."

"A . . . A . . . Agrah-Voor!" the giant said. He breathed a single long breath.

Then he spoke no more.

He trembled once, and his dark eyes closed.

"What's Agrah-Voor?" Neal asked.

KKKK! The sky turned red above them.

"Never mind that! Sparr is coming!" said Julie.

A second later, Sparr shot down from the sky. He landed on the dusty plain next to Zor.

His face was filled with anger.

His purple fins turned black.

"He doesn't look happy," Neal muttered.

The spiky points running back from the middle of Sparr's head seemed to glow bloodred.

"Ah, my Zor, my Zor! Giant man of bronze," Sparr said. "For ages you have lain asleep, waiting to do my will! And now . . ."

"Yeah, sorry he's all broken up," Eric said.

"Bring the garbage truck," Neal added.

Sparr turned. "You puny children think you have beaten me? This is just the beginning. You will never win. Now tell me what Zor said!"

Eric made a zipper motion across his mouth.

Julie shook her head and crossed her arms.

"Tell me!" Sparr commanded. "Or else."

Finally, Neal raised his hand. "Zor said . . ."

"What?" the sorcerer shrieked.

Neal frowned. "He said you should . . ."

"Yes?" the sorcerer said.

"He said you should get a life!" Neal finished.

Sparr rose up over Neal. His eyes flashed with terrible anger. "Those were your last words, you foolish child. Now, all of you, prepare to meet your doom!"

Eric gulped and turned to Neal and Julie. "Doom. That's not really a good thing, is it?"

Neal shook his head. "I'm pretty sure it's not."

Ten

One Last Thing?

Kla-blam! A bolt of blue light shot across the hills and exploded next to Sparr.

The kids turned. "Hooray!" they cheered.

Through the dust strode Galen and Keeah. Their hands were raised at Sparr. Their fingertips sizzled with blue sparks.

"Begone, Sparr!" Galen said. "You have lost!"

Eric grinned. "This just isn't your day, Sparr."

"Hrooooo!" The dragon swooped overhead.

And from the village came hundreds of Oobjas. They marched at Sparr, looking angry.

The sorcerer growled like a captive animal.

He raised his arms to the sky, flapped his cloak like a set of wings, and shot up into the air.

"Come, my Ninns," he called out bitterly. "We live to fight another day! Victory will be ours!"

Instantly, his red-faced warrior Ninns took to their groggles. The sky darkened over the dust hills as they swarmed after their leader.

Moments later, Sparr and his army were gone.

"Yahoo! We beat him!" Neal shouted, jumping up and down. "We won today! We won!"

"Excellent work, my friends," Galen said.

The giant lay motionless before them, his dark eyes crusted with dust.

"Your plan worked," Keeah said to Julie.

The Oobja king smiled broadly. "I told you she had powers. The powers of imagination!"

Julie smiled. "Well, the dragon sure helped."

Princess Keeah looked up. The dragon was perched quietly on a hill overlooking the village.

Its deep green eyes met Keeah's. An unspoken word seemed to pass between them.

Then Keeah gasped. "Oh, my gosh! Mother?"

"Hrooooo!" the dragon cried.

"I knew it!" Max chirped. "It is Queen Relna! That's why she helped us so much. My princess, the dragon is your mother!"

Keeah ran over as the blue dragon fluttered down and landed softly at the edge of the village. Keeah seemed to understand the soft, deep sounds her mother was making.

"A dragon queen," said Neal. "That is so awesome."

Galen smiled. "They are together once again."

"Families should be together," said Max.

Batamogi sniffled once. "I wish my nine brothers were here to see this day."

Julie looked at the furry king. "Wait.

Did you say *nine* brothers? You have *nine* brothers?"

Batamogi nodded. "We ruled our village together. We were all crowned at birth."

Julie blinked. "Nine brothers, nine kings, nine . . . *crowns?*"

Eric gasped at Julie. "Your dream!"

"My dream!" Julie repeated. "I was floating over a hilltop and saw nine crowns . . . oh, my gosh! I understand it now. I understand it!"

Julie ran over to Keeah and her mother. "Can your mother take us someplace?"

The dragon murmured to Keeah.

Keeah laughed. "She'd be delighted!"

Julie jumped. "Come on, everyone. King Batamogi, get ready for a family reunion!"

Everyone piled onto Queen Relna's back. Julie pointed over the hills. The queen flapped her long wings once and lifted off the ground.

"This is just like my dream," Julie said. "I was floating high over Droon."

"And you wore a crown," Neal said, tapping Julie's black helmet. "Just like you are now."

The dragon dipped over the green lake and came to rest on the hilltop where Eric, Julie, and Neal had begun their journey.

On top of the hill was the circle of nine strange trees. They stood like statues in the fading sunlight. Their tangled branches reached to the sky.

Julie turned to Batamogi. "In my dream," she said, "there were nine crowns sitting on a hilltop. Here there are nine trees. When your brothers refused to help Sparr, he must have enchanted them. He changed them. Into trees!"

"When they grabbed us, they weren't

trying to hurt us," Neal said. "They wanted us to help them!"

"There is a spell to free them," Galen said. "And Keeah, you must help me."

The two wizards joined hands. Together, they began to murmur, *"Teppi — qualem — bratoo!"*

A blue mist wrapped around the trees. The branches twitched and creaked.

The trees shrank to the size of bushes, and their leaves bunched up and became red fur. Their thick roots became squat legs. Their upper limbs became arms. Then, the circle of trees quivered together and became Batamogi's nine brothers.

"Oh, my! Oh, my!" Batamogi cried. "You see, Julie, you did help us. Now we do the dance of joy!"

The ten squat kings hugged one another. They linked arms and twirled around, laughing.

As they did, Eric turned to Galen. "Zor said one last thing before he went quiet. He said . . . Agrah-Voor."

Galen's eyes went wide. "Agrah-Voor is the legendary Land of the Lost. It is peopled by the heroes of Droon's past."

Max shivered. "They say that the only way to enter Agrah-Voor is to be a . . . a . . . ghost!"

Neal backed away. "So I guess we're not going there." He looked around. No one said a word.

"Tell me we are *not* going there!" he said.

Keeah smiled a big smile. "I think you already know the answer to that one, Neal."

He frowned. Then he shrugged. Then he smiled. "Agrah-Voor, huh? Where the ghost people live? I know what I'll dream about tonight!"

Whoosh! A cool wind blew across the dust hills. The children looked up. Hovering over a rocky ledge nearby was the magic stairway.

"It looks like our adventure is over for today," Julie said, removing her helmet. "Time to go."

Batamogi took the helmet. "We'll keep this in a place of honor, Princess. For when you return."

"I hope I do return," Julie said.

Batamogi chuckled softly and tapped his head. "Sparr was right about one thing. This is just the beginning. You'll be back. I know you will."

The three friends stepped onto the stairs.

Keeah waved to them. "Keep the magic alive!"

"You bet we will!" Eric called back.

Then the princess, the wizard, the spider troll, and the ten kings of Panjibarrh all climbed onto Queen Relna's back. The dragon circled the stairs once and headed toward the sun.

Eric, Julie, and Neal waved good-bye and started up the stairs.

Then Eric stopped.

"Wait," he said. "Why didn't the stairs work for me or Neal? I mean, it turned out that we all dreamed of Droon. But they only worked for Julie."

Neal scratched his head. "What if the stairs worked because all three of us were there?"

"That's it," said Julie. "To make the stairs work we all have to go together. Because no one is more special than anybody else. That's cool."

Neal nodded. "It's like we dreamed three parts of the same dream."

Eric thought about that for a while.

Then he smiled. "Three parts of the same dream. Cool. I can live with that."

"Me, too," Neal said. "I mean, we're a team, right?"

Julie grinned. "The absolute best."

She put up her hand.

Eric and Neal slapped her high fives. She did the same back to them.

The three friends took one more look at the land of Droon, then raced up the stairs for home.

Into the Land
of the Lost

To William Durney,
first fan of Droon,
and a wizard forever

Contents

One

A Friend in Trouble

Eric Hinkle's best friends, Neal and Julie, had just come over. But when they entered the kitchen, they found Eric and his father crawling under the counter.

"Hey, Eric, why is your head under the sink?" Neal asked as Mr. Hinkle began hammering. Then he whispered, "Did you find a new entrance to you-know-where?"

Eric laughed and stood up. "No. My dad and I are fixing this leak." He pointed to an old pipe under the sink.

Blang! Bam! His father hit the pipe.

"I guess we can't go back to Droon till you're done," said Julie softly, so Mr. Hinkle wouldn't hear.

Eric smiled. Droon was the secret world he and his friends had discovered beneath his basement.

It was a magical place of wizards and strange creatures. One of the first people they had met there was a princess named Keeah. She had become their special friend.

Galen the wizard and Max, his assistant, helped Keeah battle Lord Sparr.

Sparr, of course, was the wickedest of wicked sorcerers. He was always trying to take over Droon. Now he was searching for something called the Golden Wasp.

Galen had told them the Wasp was an object of awesome magical power.

Good thing it was hidden. For now.

Ping! Bong! Mr. Hinkle kept on hammering.

"Look at this," Julie whispered, showing Eric a silver bracelet dangling on her wrist. "I bought a little fox for my charm bracelet. It reminds me of Batamogi."

"Cool!" Eric said. On their last adventure, a fox-eared king named Batamogi had crowned Julie a princess. That sort of thing happened in Droon.

Blam! Blam! Mr. Hinkle knocked the pipes even more loudly.

"I got new socks," Neal said. "Wanna see?"

"No!" said Julie, pinching her nose.

Neal pulled off his sneakers anyway. "Bright red. I call them my Ninn socks!"

The Ninns were Sparr's soldiers. They

were chubby and angry and their skin was bright red.

"Just don't lose your socks in Droon," Eric warned. "You know what Galen says. If we ever leave anything behind, something from Droon will come here. And something from here will go there."

Just then, Eric's dad stopped banging, stood up, and sighed. "I'm not quite sure what's wrong," he said.

Neal nudged Eric aside and stooped under the sink. "Turn that nozzle," he said, pointing. "You need to release the pressure or it will explode."

Mr. Hinkle frowned. "Are you sure?"

Neal nodded. "My dad does plumbing stuff all the time. That nozzle turns."

Mr. Hinkle tried it. "It won't budge. What am I doing wrong?"

"Listening to Neal," Julie said with a

chuckle. "Now put your sneakers back on, Neal."

"Yes, princess!" he said, scowling.

"Wait, I think it's moving —" Mr. Hinkle said. The nozzle squeaked — *err-err-err!* — then *POP!* It exploded under the sink. Water burst from the pipe and onto the kitchen floor.

"Wet socks!" Neal cried. "I hate wet socks!"

"The pipe broke!" Mr. Hinkle shouted. "Holy cow! We need a towel. Eric, get me a wrench! Everybody out of the way!"

The kids shot down to the basement for a wrench.

"There's water everywhere," Neal said. "Your mom's going to be really mad!"

"Neal, will you just —" Eric started, then he stopped. Julie was standing at the tool bench. Her eyes were wide with wonder.

And with fear.

In her hands was not a wrench, but the soccer ball that Keeah had cast a spell on. It was supposed to tell them when they were needed in Droon.

And now, across the surface of the ball words appeared in thin blue ink.

NOORD PLEH, EM PLEH, PSAW
NEDLOG EHT
SKEES RRAPS

"Eric-c-c-c!" sputtered his father from the kitchen above.

"We're looking for the wrench, Dad!" Eric called up.

Neal pulled his shoes on, took the ball, and quickly reversed the letters in his head. *Sparr seeks the Golden Wasp, help me, help Droon.*

"I knew it!" said Julie. "We'll help your

dad when we get back. But we have to help Keeah first! She's in big trouble!"

Eric nodded. Time ran differently in Droon. He knew they would be back before anyone missed them.

They shoved aside the large carton that blocked the door beneath the stairs. They jammed themselves inside a small closet. Julie shut the door. Eric flicked off the closet light.

Whoosh! Instantly, the floor vanished beneath them and they stood at the top of a long, shimmering staircase.

The magical staircase to the land of Droon.

Eric took the first step. Then another and another. His friends followed close behind.

The air was pink all around them.

At the bottom of the stairs was a rocky plain stretching for miles in every direction. Boulders lay scattered like pebbles tossed by a giant.

Eric wondered if maybe they had been.

"Welcome to the middle of nowhere," Julie said.

As the stairs faded into the pink air, a plume of dust rose from the horizon. The ground thundered with beating hooves.

"It's a pilka!" Julie cried out, pointing to a shaggy-haired beast with six legs galloping toward them. "It's Galen's pilka, Leep. And Keeah and Max are riding her! They're coming this way."

"So is he!" said Eric, pointing to a big flying lizard, diving down from the sky.

"A groggle!" Neal said. "This is not good."

The groggle swooped down at the pilka. On its back was a single rider, a man dressed in a long black cloak. Two purple fins stuck up behind his ears, and a row of spikes ran back from his high forehead. His eyes burned like fire.

"Uh-oh," said Julie. "It's . . . it's . . ."

". . . Lord Sparr!" Eric cried.

"Wet socks *and* Lord Sparr?" Neal groaned. "Already my day is ruined!"

Two

Under Sparr's Spell

Leep skidded to a halt and Keeah tumbled to the ground, out of breath.

"Sparr will stop at nothing," she gasped.

"And he has a terrible new weapon," said Max, Galen's spider-troll helper. His orange hair stood straight up. His big eyes blinked fearfully.

Kkkk! The sky crackled. Lord Sparr swooped down on them like a bird of prey.

"Princess Keeah!" Sparr snarled, leaping from his groggle and planting himself before her. "Tell me now! Where is my Golden Wasp?"

"She will never tell you!" Max cried fiercely.

"And you have to deal with us!" Eric shouted.

"Puny troublemakers," Sparr sneered. "Begone!"

Ka-blam! He scattered the friends with a bolt of fiery light from his fingertips.

Max was flung back across the dust like a bowling ball. When he stopped rolling, his eight legs were twisted and tied in a knot.

"My magic orb will make you speak!" Sparr said to Keeah. He pulled a black glass ball from his cloak and tossed it into the air. Strange designs were etched into the ball. It glowed as it hung over Keeah's head.

"Don't look at it!" Julie cried out.

"Ha!" snarled Sparr. "The more you try not to look, the more you *must* look. . . ."

He was right. Keeah tried to look away but could not. She stared into the orb's bright center.

"The Wasp . . ." she murmured, her voice strangely different, "lies hidden in . . ."

"Keeah, no!" Neal shouted. "Don't tell him —"

". . . Agrah-Voor," she whispered.

"Ah!" Sparr cried. "How fitting that I should *find* my Wasp in the Land of the *Lost*! Come, princess, let's go there together."

Sparr tore the floating orb out of the air.

"Oh, no you don't!" Eric shouted, leaping at him.

Kkkk! A sudden burst of light from the orb struck Eric in the face. The ball's crisscrossed jagged lines flashed brightly in his eyes. "Ah!" he cried, falling to the ground.

Sparr jumped up onto his groggle. "Princess, come!"

Without protesting, Keeah mounted the beast and sat behind him.

"We'll follow you!" Julie yelled, rushing to Eric.

Sparr's lips curled into a smile. "Such good friends. And now, a little fun!"

From another pocket in his cloak, Sparr pulled out a handful of wiggling things.

"What are those?" said Neal. "Worms? So, you brought your family along?"

Sparr scattered the worms on the ground. They grew long and thick and began to hiss. Soon the ground was swarming with them.

"Snakes, go forth!" Sparr boomed.

Hissing loudly, the snakes headed out across the plain.

Sparr grinned coldly. "Just a little something to keep old Galen busy!"

The sorcerer pulled sharply on the reins and dug his heels into the groggle's sides. The beast left the ground. Princess Keeah clung to the sorcerer's saddle, her eyes blank.

A moment later, they were gone.

Julie helped Eric to his feet. "Are you okay?"

Eric rubbed his eyes. "I saw lines. Squiggly lines. That design on the ball burned into my eyes. Man, that hurt. The light blinded me."

"Ooh, that Sparr!" Max growled. "I'll teach him a lesson! Well, I would if Galen were here. Oh, I wish —"

Z-z-z-z! Suddenly, the air blurred, and a blue mist spun around them, streaked with blue light.

Z-z-z-zamm! A figure appeared before them, as the light continued to spin.

"Galen!" Julie exclaimed.

It was Galen, first wizard of Droon. He wore a long blue robe covered with stars and moons. His white beard trailed nearly to his waist. He was bending over, digging in his pockets.

"Master!" Max said, scrambling up to him. "It's bad. Sparr has —"

Galen stood up. "No need to tell me. Sparr has loosed his slithery snakes all across Droon. I must uncharm them one by one. That is why *you* must go to Agrah-Voor!"

"We're ready," said Eric, the pain in his eyes lessening. "Which way?"

"Not so fast," said the wizard, rummaging in his pockets again. "Agrah-Voor is the city of ghosts. It is the abode of the fallen heroes of Droon."

"So it's where the dead people live?" asked Neal.

"Just so," said Galen. "No living soul can harm another there. But there is a worse danger. You must be gone by midnight or all will be lost."

Eric noticed that the blue air continued to spin around as they talked. Were they . . . moving?

"What happens at midnight?" Julie asked.

The wizard frowned. "If midnight finds you in the city walls, you will become ghosts, too."

Neal gulped loud enough for everyone to hear. "Then . . . I think we'd better get started!"

Galen smiled. "Take this." He handed Neal a small hourglass. "It will tell you when to leave Agrah-Voor. The last grains will fall on the stroke of midnight."

Neal watched the tiny sand grains fall from the top of the glass to the bottom. No matter which way he turned the glass, the sand always ran in the same direction. "Now I know what they mean when they say that time is running out."

The air continued to spin around them as Galen pulled something else from his robes. "Take this, also," he said, handing Julie a small mirror in a silver frame. "Rub its surface when you need to speak with me. I, too, shall carry one. But you may use it only once."

"I'll take good care of it," said Julie, slipping the mirror into her pocket.

"What will Sparr do if he finds the Wasp?" Eric asked.

"The Golden Wasp controls the mind," the wizard said darkly. "It can make people forget. Turn them against their loved ones.

Change who they are forever. Sparr will become even more powerful."

To Eric, the wizard had never before seemed so serious nor looked so sad.

"Now," said Galen, "the quickest way to Agrah-Voor is across the Bridge of Mists. Even Sparr doesn't know this way yet. If you hurry, you can get there before him. And . . . here we are!"

Poof! The spinning blue air vanished.

Before them stood a stone bridge. Its near side was clearly visible. Its far side was shrouded in fog.

"Now go," said Galen. "I'm off to fight snakes!" An instant later — *zamm!* — the wizard was gone.

Eric looked at his friends. He could tell they were as scared as he was. Scared for themselves.

Scared for Princess Keeah.

Scared of ghosts.

"Let's do it," he said, trying to sound brave.

Julie, Neal, and Max nodded in agreement.

The thick mist poured around them as they stepped up onto the bridge.

Three

Bridge of Mists

"Now I know why they call Agrah-Voor the Land of the Lost," Neal said as the fog rolled over him. "You get lost just getting there!"

"Good one," said Eric, squinting to see him. "Everyone keep talking, so we don't lose each other."

Max scampered across Julie's feet. "I'm sorry about all of this," he said. "I should have protected Keeah much better. I'm not very good."

"Don't be silly," Julie replied, scruffing his orange hair. "It's not *your* fault. Sparr is a major sorcerer. Plus he's got that wicked black ball thingie. We'll find Keeah. Don't worry."

Soon the fog began to thin. Rocky walls surrounded them. Long pointy formations hung from a ceiling they couldn't see. Water splashed on the craggy stone floor.

"Somehow, we've gone underground," Eric whispered. "This is a cavern. A wet one. There's a picture like this in our science book."

"I smell something burning," said Max.

"That means people, right?" Eric said.

"Or maybe ghosts," Neal whispered.

A pale light shone from up ahead. Two

torches stuck out from the cavern wall, sputtering.

"We are not the first ones to travel this way," said Max. Then he stopped and pointed. "Look."

Beyond the torches was a short set of steps cut into the rock. The bottom step was underwater.

In the water was a boat.

"Wow!" said Julie. "It looks like something from a fairy tale! Or a dream."

The boat was painted yellow and blue, and each end curved up away from the water.

"If we're supposed to take that," Neal said, "it better float. My socks are just starting to dry."

Max clambered into the boat first. "There are no oars and no sail. I wonder how it moves."

When Julie stepped in, the odd little boat wobbled slightly, then became still.

Neal pulled the small hourglass from his pocket. "I guess we'd better hurry. These grains of sand aren't running any slower." He stepped in, too.

Slap. Slap. Eric turned to look back up the stairs. "Did you hear something?"

"Only my heartbeat," said Julie.

Eric stepped in. The moment he did, the boat pulled away from the dock. "Yikes! It's magic!"

"It's Droon," Neal said softly.

Eric gazed down at the black surface of the water. He wondered if it was cool or warm. He wondered if it even *was* water.

He dipped his hand in.

He gasped.

As his fingers touched the water, the

surface glistened for an instant, then turned crystal clear.

"I can see through it!" Julie exclaimed. "There's a . . . a . . ."

"A city!" Neal said.

It *was* a city. A tangle of odd buildings twisted up from the ground below. Eric could make out a high wall around them. "Is that Agrah-Voor?" he asked.

"Where the dead people live?" Neal added.

"It is the city of ghosts," Max chittered.

Suddenly, Eric's ears twitched. "Ninns! I heard them before. Now I'm sure of it. Ninns are coming!"

The next noise they heard was the sound of heavy feet slapping the stones.

"There they are!" Julie whispered as a band of fat red Ninns tramped down to the water.

"Augh! Small ones!" one cried out. "Stop!"

Thwang! Sploosh! A flaming arrow whizzed past the boat, splashed the water, bounced, and clattered against the stone bank on the far side.

"We cannot be captured!" Max urged. They all began to splash at the water.

"Both hands, Eric!" cried Neal. "If I become a ghost, my mom's really going to be mad!"

Thwang! Another Ninn arrow shot so close to Eric's ear, he could feel the flame's heat.

"I stop boat!" one Ninn grunted as he chased them along the bank. "I stop boat!"

"I have a better idea!" Julie yelled. "How about you just *stop*!"

But he shot his arrow, and it struck its mark.

Thwang! Crrrack! The arrow's tip struck

the hull just below the waterline. A thin stream of water spurted into the boat.

"A leak!" Max cried. "We've sprung a leak!"

"Neal, your socks," said Eric. "We need them to plug the hole!"

"My . . . new . . . socks?"

"No!" Julie cried. She pulled Eric's hands from the hole. "We need to sink so we can escape!"

"Oh, man, oh, man!" Neal groaned.

The small boat tipped forward as it took on more water.

The last thing anyone heard before the boat went down was Neal saying, "Glub! Glub!"

Four

Thief of Agrah-Voor

Silvery water rushed over the kids. Eric gulped for air as the boat went down. He hoped he could hold his breath for as long as it would take —

Suddenly — *whoosh!* — it was over and they were in air again. Flying *below* the water.

Cool air fluttered over them as the boat floated slowly toward the ground below. It seemed as if the boat were protected by invisible parachutes.

"Our clothes are dry," Julie said.

"Even my socks!" Neal said. "This is weird."

"This is Agrah-Voor," Max said.

Eric looked up. The river they had just passed through was like a thin stripe across the sky. Above that was the cavern and the Ninns peering down from it.

"Look at them," Max chirped happily. "Staring at us like numbskulls, tugging their chins!"

It was good to hear Max laugh, Eric thought. Even though he knew Max was worried about Keeah. And about Sparr and the Golden Wasp.

And it wouldn't be long before the Ninns stopped staring and started following.

The boat floated down and thudded

gently on the ground outside the giant city wall. They climbed out. The ground was hard and dusty.

"We did it," said Julie. "We actually got here."

"But we're on the wrong side of the wall," said Neal. "How are we going to get in?"

Before anyone could answer — swoosh! — something flashed down the wall at them.

A figure dressed in green, swinging on a rope.

"Aeee!" cried the creature, crashing into the kids. Neal and Eric tumbled backward over Max. Julie went spinning to the ground.

"Hey! He stole my mirror!" Julie cried. She sprang up at him, but he twisted away and scrambled back up the rope. "Rope, up!" he said.

"Stop him!" Julie yelped.

With one strong leap, Max jumped to the rope and pushed the creature off. Neal tackled him as he tried to jump away. Eric pounced and pinned the creature's arms firmly to the ground.

"I give up! You win!" came a high-pitched squeal.

The creature had a face something like a rat's, with a long pointed snout and whiskers. His arms were long and muscular, his legs bowed and short like a monkey's. He was dressed in a silky green tunic and wore a leather pack on his shoulder. His slippers curled up at the ends.

When the kids released him, he jumped to his feet and bowed. "Allow me to introduce myself. I am Shago, chief thief of Agrah-Voor. My fingers were made for grabbing, my arms for —"

"Just give it back!" Julie demanded,

setting her face in a fierce scowl and holding out her hand. "That's Galen's mirror. And if he finds out —"

"Galen!" Shago's whiskers curled sharply. "Oh! First wizard of Droon? Oh! Why didn't you say so?" He smiled so widely his ears wiggled. Tugging the mirror from his leather sack, he handed it back to Julie. "Queen Hazad speaks of Galen often. Oh! He is one of the great heroes of Droon!"

"Galen sent us here to help Princess Keeah," Eric said. "Who is Queen Hazad?"

Shago snorted. "None other than the ruler of Agrah-Voor! Come. I will take you to her —"

Splash! The silvery water above broke open suddenly. Ninn soldiers were jumping into the river and splashing through it into the sky, just as the kids had done.

"The Ninns are following us," Julie said. "We'd better move it! Fast!"

Shago snorted again as he tugged sharply on his rope. "Fat Ninns. They'll make craters when they land! Come, then. Follow! Follow!"

Shago's voice squeaked when he grew excited. But beneath his whiskers was a smile Eric liked.

"Follow!" Shago repeated, racing to the great wall. "Unless you'd rather chat with Ninns?"

"If I have a choice," said Neal, scrambling after the thief, "I think we'll follow you. Fast!"

But he couldn't. None of them could.

For when Shago reached the foot of the wall, he mumbled some words, then slipped quietly, smoothly, and impossibly right through the thick stone wall.

"Holy crow!" Eric exclaimed, jerking to a stop. "I think we just met our first . . . ghost!"

Five

The Ghost Queen

"Ghost or not," said Julie, "Shago's the only one who can help us now! Shago! Come back!"

Flump! Boing! The Ninns bounced to the earth, jumped upright, then rushed at the kids.

"Oh, man!" Neal gasped. "Hey, Shago!"

The thief's face popped up above the .wall. "Why didn't you follow me?" he called down.

"We're not ghosts!" Julie yelled up. "Yet!"

"But we soon will be," Eric said, "if you don't send down your rope!"

"Rope, down!" Shago's rope unwound down the wall and dropped at the kids' feet. The moment the kids touched it, it began to pull them up. Soon they were standing at the top of the wall.

"My magic rope!" Shago said, beaming. "I stole it from a witch. But you must not think I'm a ghost."

"But you walked right through that wall!" Neal said.

The thief chuckled. "I snitched a magician's spell book once. Learned a trick or two. No, no. Only heroes of battle live in Agrah-Voor."

"Then why are you here?" Julie asked.

Shago's tiny brown eyes grew moist.

"My family is here. They are the true ghosts."

Boom! Boom! The Ninns were pounding at the walls.

"We must tell the queen," said Shago. "Rope, down!" The rope tossed itself down into the city.

Eric couldn't believe the view as they descended. Agrah-Voor was a city of twisted turrets and crooked towers, of purple stones and dark banners, of winding alleys and narrow streets. At its center was an enormous fountain.

Julie pointed to a large wooden gate. "Is that the way out?" she asked.

Shago nodded. "The Gate of Life. When Droon is at peace again, the ghosts will leave through the gate. They will live again. Alas, it has been sealed for many years."

"Because of Lord Sparr?" said Julie.

Shago gritted his teeth. "The evil one himself."

They swung lower into a crisscross tangle of streets.

"How can you tell where you are?" Neal asked. "These streets go every which way."

Shago smiled back at him. "The pipes," he said, pointing to a spidery maze of water pipes running along the ground below. "The pipes lead from the outer wall to the fountain. At the fountain we shall find our queen!"

Neal nudged Eric. "Good thing there's not a leak in one of *those* pipes!"

"If there were, we wouldn't let you fix it," said Julie.

Shago twitched his whiskers, and the rope touched the ground.

They entered a broad paved yard the size of a football field. The fountain in the middle spouted crystal water. All around it were men and women and creatures of all kinds dressed in leather and armor of every color.

Some warriors hurled large rocks to one another. Others clanged old swords against rusted suits of armor, sending off sparks. Still others ran footraces around the edges of the square.

"The heroes of Droon!" Shago whispered. "Keeping in shape for when they live again."

"They don't look like ghosts to me," Neal said. "Pretty colorful. Are they really, you know . . ."

"They are dead," said Shago. "But they wake each day hoping that today Droon will be at peace. As the hours wear on, they lose their hope, their color, their life. By nightfall, you'll see. They'll be different."

With those mysterious words, Shago led them to a large wooden throne. Pillow-shaped purple Lumpies stood at attention on either side. On the throne sat an old woman.

"Queen Hazad," said Shago softly, bowing.

Queen Hazad was beautiful but very old. She wore a crown, but it did not sparkle like most crowns do. It was oddly shaped, as if it were made of thick branches of wood.

But the queen's cheeks were rosy, and she wore a bright orange gown.

"My cane, please," the queen said. An old spider troll scampered up with a carved stick.

"Welcome," the queen said, hobbling over to the kids. "I sense you do not bring good news. We do not often get visitors, you know."

Eric bowed. "Sorry," he said. "I'm Eric. These are my friends Julie, Neal, and Max. Sparr has captured Princess Keeah and is bringing her here. Galen sent us to help her — and to warn you about something else."

"Sparr knows the Golden Wasp is here," said Julie. "He's mad and he wants it back."

"So the Ninns are trying to bust down the wall," Neal added. "They sort of followed us."

The queen drew in a sharp breath. Her cheeks seemed to grow slightly paler. "Guards!"

The warriors jousting with the suits of armor hustled over. "My queen!" they said.

"Gather my people," the queen said. "Agrah-Voor is under attack." The guards raced off.

The queen turned to the kids. "Sparr

cannot harm you or Princess Keeah. But you cannot stay long."

"That's why we're here," said Eric. "And to keep Sparr from getting the Wasp."

"The Golden Wasp!" the queen said, as if remembering something painful from the distant past. "It is a cursed thing with a sting that can turn love to hate, beauty to ugliness, life to death."

The kids shivered as she described the Wasp.

"Long ago, Galen charmed it and hid it," the queen went on, "but its power could not remain hidden for long. Sparr battled me for the Wasp. I kept him from it but lost my life. I took the Wasp with me when I came here. For so many years it has remained a secret."

Ka-blam! Lightning flashed across the sky.

"Until now," said Julie.

"Sparr has broken the wall!" a guard reported.

As the man spoke, more color left the old queen's cheeks. And not only her cheeks. The bright robes she wore seemed to turn gray, the color of ashes.

As Ninns thundered through the streets, other warriors began to turn pale, too.

Eric shivered with fear. He knew what that meant. Their hope was leaving them.

"Oh! Oh!" Shago cried nervously. "I am a thief, not a warrior. I must hide!" He scampered away quickly.

An instant later, the square was swarming with Ninns. Lord Sparr swept in with them. Keeah was held by two Ninns. She was still in a trance.

"Where is the Golden Wasp?" Sparr demanded, the fins behind his ears flaring red. "Tell me, Queen Hazad, or I shall tear your city apart!"

"I shall never tell you!" the queen replied.

"Then Princess Keeah herself shall become a ghost!"

Six

Walls of Terror

The sorcerer roughly pulled Keeah to the center of the square.

As the princess stood there, silent, unmoving, Sparr pulled the black orb from his cloak and tossed it in the air above her.

"What is he doing now?" Max whispered.

"I don't know." Eric still felt the pain in his head where the orb had struck him with its light. "But I am really getting to not like that thing."

Eric stepped forward. "Sparr, let Keeah go! You can't harm her here, so why even try?"

"Yeah," Neal snarled, moving up behind Eric. "Why not crawl back where you came from?"

The sorcerer turned slowly. The fins behind his ears became black with anger. "You will not talk so bravely when I march into your Upper World to fulfill my mission!"

Mission? thought Eric. *What mission?*

Sparr then pointed his fingers at the hovering ball and muttered some words under his breath.

"Leave our princess alone, Sparr!" the queen shouted.

Sparr's eyes flashed. "Oh, yes! I'll leave

your princess alone. She'll be all alone. In-side!"

"Inside what?" Eric demanded.

"Inside . . . this!"

With that, the ball flooded its light around Keeah.

Suddenly — *fwang!* A wall burst up from the ground behind the princess. It was ten feet high and jagged across the top.

Sparr laughed. "Keeah . . . awake!"

The princess blinked, then looked around her. "Where am I?"

"In your new home!" Sparr replied. "Orb . . . continue!"

Fwang! A second wall burst up next to her. Another shot up on the other side. A fourth wall in front closed her off.

"Stop!" said the queen.

But the walls kept coming.

Some walls curved in, some bent out,

but all of them twisted and tangled around Keeah until she was entirely hidden by them.

"A maze!" Julie gasped. "Sparr is building a maze. Keeah will never find her way out!"

Fwang! As the last jagged wall jolted into place, the square fell into silence. The maze was complete. Its walls filled the square.

Sparr laughed. "I may not be able to harm your princess. But there is only one path through this maze. Only the orb knows what it is. It will take her days to find it. Weeks, maybe. Perhaps never! If your princess ever stumbles out, she will be . . . a ghost!"

"We'll get her out!" Julie said firmly. "You can't stop us!"

Sparr's lips curled into a nasty smile. "I

have no intention of stopping you. You'll stay to help your friend. And you will become ghosts, too! Ha-ha! I can see you getting pale already!"

His fat soldiers gargled with laughter.

Then the sorcerer whirled around. "With these troublemaking children out of the way, I am free to find my Wasp. Ninns! Tear this city apart! Queen Hazad, you will wish you had given me what I seek."

At Sparr's command, the Ninns began breaking everything in sight, trying to find the hidden Wasp. The ghosts tried to stop them, but the Ninns tore fiercely through the streets beyond the square.

The children stood alone before the maze.

"Keeah-eeah-eeah!" Julie shouted, her voice echoing inside the black walls.

The sounds of fighting echoed in their

ears, too. Max began to whimper as he paced in front of the maze. "What to do? What to do?"

Eric felt his spirits sink. Without even checking Galen's hourglass, he knew. There was no way to get Keeah out in time. Sparr would find the Wasp and become even more powerful. And their friend would be stuck in the Land of the Lost forever.

And yet, something about the huge maze seemed . . . familiar to Eric.

How could that be?

The maze was huge. Sparr said there was only one way to the center, but no one knew the way.

No one.

No one?

Seven

In the Mind's Eye

As Eric stared at the maze before him, he was sure he had seen it before.

"That's impossible," he said out loud.

"No kidding it's impossible," said Neal, checking the wizard's hourglass. "We'll never find her in time. Prepare to be ghosts, people. My mom's going to be really mad now!"

"No," said Eric. "I mean, I've seen this maze before, but I couldn't have."

Eric's head began to ache. It was the same pain he had felt when the glass ball shot him with its light. It still hurt. . . .

It still hurt.

"Oh, my gosh!" he gasped. "The lines! The squiggly lines when the orb's light blasted me. The design on the ball is the same as the maze!"

Julie blinked. "Do you *know* the way in?"

Eric closed his eyes. He suddenly felt helpless. And dumb. "I see some of the design, the crisscrossing walls, but not the whole thing."

"Galen could unlock your mind," Max said. "If he were here. But, of course, he's not —"

Julie nearly jumped. "The mirror! We can call Galen!" She pulled the wizard's magic mirror from her pocket and quickly rubbed the surface.

Galen's face appeared. "Ah! My friends. King Zello and I are keeping the spider trolls safe from Sparr's snakes. What news?"

"Sparr created a terrible maze from his evil orb," said Julie. "Keeah is locked inside."

"And Eric thinks he knows the way in," said Neal. "He's seen it before. Only he doesn't remember all of it."

"We must release his memory," said Max.

"Eric, come closer," the wizard said, waving his hand. A swirling light shone in the glass. "I will put you to sleep. When you awake, you will see the maze in your mind's eye."

"I'm ready," said Eric.

"You are sleepy," Galen droned softly. "Very sleepy. Your eyelids are getting heavy. Heavy."

Eric stared into the swirling light. His mind drifted. He felt sleepy.

He knew Galen was speaking to him, but he wasn't sure of the words. He felt as if he were falling. Then, all of a sudden, he bolted upright.

His eyes were open. The mirror was blank.

"Huh? What happened?" he said.

"I think you were hypnotized," said Julie. "Do you remember anything? Think, Eric. Think."

Eric closed his eyes. He tried to silence all the sounds. The distant swords clanging against one another. The grunting Ninns, the yelling ghosts.

If the sounds disappeared, maybe he could —

Enter.

He blinked. "Who said that?"

Neal gave him a look. "Said what? You're the only one talking."

Enter. Then go left three paces.

Eric entered the maze.

Neal turned to Max. "Maybe you should weave a spider-silk thread as we go. So we can find the entrance again."

Max's eyes brightened. "Good plan, Neal."

He shrugged. "I get one, every now and then."

"Three paces left," said Eric. "Then turn —"

Right, left, straight, left, back again, two rights, a sharp zigzag. It seemed to take hours to thread their way between the jagged black walls.

But Eric did not make a false move. Every turn, every angle, every crisscrossed line of the orb stood out clearly in his mind.

Then, finally, they took one sharp right turn and came face-to-face with a blank wall.

"What?" he said. He closed his eyes again.

He saw the wall there, too.

What happened? What was going on?

"No pressure or anything," said Neal. "But we're losing time here."

Eric put his hands on the wall. It was cold. Night was falling in Agrah-Voor. Soon after that it would be midnight. He suddenly felt very afraid. Afraid that Keeah would be trapped. Afraid that he had taken them the wrong way. Afraid that they would become ghosts — and it would be all his fault.

"This isn't right," he murmured, swallowing his fear. He retraced his steps. "Back up. . . ."

Julie shot a fearful look at Max as they

backed into a small space. "This isn't the way we came."

"Uh-oh," Neal mumbled. "Wrong turn."

"Quiet!" Eric studied the lines burned into his memory. No, he wasn't wrong. He wasn't.

He traced his way back to the wall again. He pressed against it. It began to move.

"Keeah?" he whispered.

Then, there she was, falling into them. The wall slid away as Eric spoke her name.

"Eric! Julie! Neal! Max!" she cried, nearly weeping with joy.

Max bounced up and down. "My princess!"

The sounds of battle thundered around them.

"Party later, people," said Julie. "Sparr is still hunting for his dumb Wasp. The ghosts need us."

Keeah trembled. Then she narrowed her eyes in defiance. "We must stop him!"

They followed Max's silken thread out of the maze. The sounds of fighting drew them farther and farther into the tangle of streets.

Many buildings lay in ruins.

"Oh, woe!" cried a ghost, stumbling past them.

Eric recognized him as one of the warriors tossing rocks earlier. Now he could barely support his own weight. It was as if smoke had taken shape as a person.

"The heroes have lost hope," said Eric. "Just like Shago said. By the end of the day they really are no more than ghosts."

"They're afraid they'll be in Agrah-Voor forever," Julie added.

"They won't be," said Keeah, "if I can help it."

Carefully, they entered a small square

surrounded by crooked towers. They dashed behind a pile of rubble and peeked over the top.

The ghosts and Ninns had fought to a standstill. Now Lord Sparr towered over the old queen.

"We are destroying your city stone by stone," Sparr snarled. "But now I believe that one of *you* is hiding my Golden Wasp. If you won't surrender it, you shall all perish!"

"You know no living soul can harm us!" the queen said.

The sorcerer cackled. "No *living* soul . . . yes. I've thought of that. Ninns! Bring in the box!"

Eric turned to Keeah. "Is that a new weapon? A box? Filled with what?"

"Probably not chocolate," said Neal.

Six Ninns dragged in a large black box. Their faces grew even redder as they huffed and puffed with the effort. Finally, they dropped it with a thud, tugged off the top, then scattered fearfully.

"What's inside?" Julie asked.

On the box was strange old writing.

"Oh, no!" Keeah gasped. "I hope it's not . . ."

"I'm afraid it is," Max whimpered softly when he saw. "The Warriors of the Skorth!"

Eight

Warriors of the Skorth

"Arise, O Skorth!" Sparr boomed over the box. Then he began to mumble strange words, as if he were casting a spell.

Suddenly, there came a scraping, clacking sound from inside the box. Then something jumped out. It clattered to the ground.

"Holy crow!" Eric gasped. "A . . . bone!"

Then another bone flew out. Then another and another. Soon the air was filled with bones jumping out of the box.

"Stop this, Sparr!" the queen demanded. Her ghostly people crowded around her.

The sorcerer ignored her.

"Arise!" he said again, and the loose bones began to form a skeleton.

Two feet assembled themselves. They attached to legs. A spine wobbled up, then two arms flung themselves from the bone pile. Fingers clattered into place. Finally, a skull flew up and sat on the neck.

The whole thing wiggled once, clacked its jaws, and stood at attention. Sparr laughed.

"I really don't like when he laughs," Neal said. "Because it's usually not so funny."

"It's not funny this time, either," said Keeah. "We need to do something."

"Definitely," Eric said, gulping. "But what?"

Eight more skeleton warriors flew up just as the first had done. Then they pulled armor and weapons from the box.

Some Skorth wore thick armor. Others were bareheaded, showing their bony skulls, their grinning jaws. But all had spears with blades that whirled and spun wildly.

They stood awaiting Sparr's command.

"Living souls cannot harm you, dear queen?" Sparr said with a laugh. "Behold the Warriors of the Skorth! As dead as dead can be! From ancient times, their only purpose has been to destroy. If you won't surrender the Wasp to me, you will surrender it to them!"

With that, Sparr cast his black ball into the air.

Zzzz! As it hung there, the orb shed light down on the ghosts.

The queen and her soldiers shuddered once, then became still.

"Sparr is putting them in a trance," Keeah whispered. "Just as he did to me."

"That's enough!" Eric whispered. "These ghosts need to defend themselves. I'm gonna blast that evil baseball out of the park!"

"How?" asked Neal. "It's twenty feet high!"

Eric wasn't sure. As he thought, he caught sight of a dark shape moving among the Ninns. While Sparr continued to mumble over the Skorth, Shago was sneaking around, stealing things from the Ninns.

Eric grinned. "Shago! I knew he couldn't disappear. Not with so many things to snitch!"

"Yes," said Julie. "Rope . . . here!"

Instantly, the magic rope, which was still wound on Shago's shoulder, tugged him across the ground to where the kids were.

Floop! Shago fell down behind the mound.

"My friends! Look what I have! A Ninn bow!"

"Shago, we need your help," Eric said.

He grumbled. "I am a thief, not a hero."

"Here's your chance to be both," said Keeah.

"I've got a plan," Eric said. As he explained it, Shago's ears flicked with delight.

"I can do that!" he said. Then, looking both ways, he scampered out from behind the mound. A minute later, he came back with a thin carved stick. He gave it to Eric.

Julie blinked. "Is that Queen Hazad's cane?"

Shago grumbled. "There are a hundred Ninns here. It's all I could find."

The thief scampered off. So did Eric.

Sparr finished mumbling his magic words.

"Now, go, Skorth. Destroy every ghost if you have to. But find my Golden Wasp!"

Clack! Clack! The skeletons turned and marched toward the defenseless ghosts.

Sparr began to laugh. "This will be good —"

"You don't know what good is, Sparr!" Eric cried from the summit of one tower. "Shago?"

"Up here!" Shago stood atop another tower, the Ninn bow in his hands. "My family are ghosts because of you, Sparr! Now I'll return the favor!"

Thwang! His flaming arrow flew at Sparr. The sorcerer leaped out of the way.

Then Julie, Neal, Keeah, and Max started hurling stones at the Skorth.

Finally, Eric leaped from his tower, clutching the magic rope in one hand and the queen's cane in the other. "Rope! To that ball!" he cried.

As the rope carried him across the square, Eric took a swing at the glowing orb.

"He swings —" Julie shouted.

Crash! The orb shattered into a million pieces, shooting light everywhere.

"— and it's outta there!" Neal whooped.

The queen stirred. The ghosts raised their swords at the skeletons, ready to fight.

But the orb's final blast of light sizzled up and down the length of the queen's cane as Eric swung it.

"Ahh!" he screamed, dropping the cane.

"It burned me!" He slid from the rope and landed in the square, clutching his hand.

The Skorth advanced once more.

"Stop!" the sorcerer suddenly bellowed. The whole square fell into silence. The cane lay at Sparr's feet. "Can it be?" he said.

Sparr waved his hand over it. The cane turned gold and began to shrink. It sprouted wings. One end became a flat triangular head. The rest formed the stomach and legs . . . of a wasp.

A wasp six inches long.

A wasp made entirely of gold.

"My terrible power!" Sparr shouted. "It's you! I have you again!"

The Golden Wasp began to buzz and whine, its wings flicking and fluttering quickly. The sorcerer pulled an iron glove from his cloak. Before the wasp could fly away, Sparr clasped his gloved hand around it.

Suddenly, Shago yelled out, "You shall not have it!" He leaped down at Sparr, but the sorcerer flung him to the ground. Sparr snatched Shago's leather sack and plunged the Wasp into it.

"Skorth, destroy them. Destroy them all!" Sparr growled hoarsely, clutching the sack. "Come, my Ninns! Let us leave this place. Agrah-Voor is the Land of the Lost. Today — we have won!"

His Ninns followed, grunting and howling. In a moment, they were gone.

The ghosts stood in one line, the skeleton men in another. The Skorth clacked their bony jaws. Then they aimed their spinning spears — *whrrr!*

"I think they plan to kill us," Julie said, backing up.

"I suddenly have another plan!" Neal said.

"The one where we run real fast?" Eric asked.

"That's the one!" Neal said.

Nine

Against the Gate of Life

"Ghosts of Agrah-Voor, to battle!" cried Queen Hazad. "These children are the future of Droon!"

Whrrr! The Skorth lunged at the children, but the ghosts struck back, wielding the swords they'd used when they were alive. Even Queen Hazad grabbed a wooden club and swung it swiftly.

Clang! Boom! The sounds of fighting filled the city.

Eric felt his heart race to see the old men and women stride into battle.

"We fight for Droon!" one ghost woman yelled out, her hands grasping an ancient sword.

"For Droon!" the others shouted, as if it were their old battle cry.

"Quickly!" the queen shouted to the kids. "Shago, take them to the Gate of Life. We will try to hold off the Skorth and meet you there."

"Are you sure the gate will open?" Keeah asked.

"It is the only way!" the queen said. "Hurry!"

Without another word, the four kids and Max followed Shago into the nearest alley. The thief wove a zigzag path through the narrow streets.

Eric could tell he was following the water pipes out to the wall.

Soon, they came to a huge wooden drawbridge, nearly as tall as the wall itself.

"The Gate of Life," said Shago. "But the hinges froze and the chains rusted long ago."

"It's huge!" Julie said. "We'll never get it open. Not in a million years."

"How about in ten minutes?" Neal asked, gazing at the wizard's miniature hourglass. "Because that's all we have before the sand runs out."

Clang! Whrrr! The sounds of battle flooded out of the narrow streets. A moment later, the Skorth charged out of an alley, grinning.

"Man, it's creepy when they smile," Neal said, backing away.

"I guess they like their job," said Julie.

The ghosts poured in, but the Skorth were fast. Eric turned to run, then tripped on a water pipe.

A Skorth warrior charged at him.

"Eric!" Keeah cried, rushing over. She pushed him away just in time.

Clang! Splursh! The spear's whirring blades struck one of the water pipes and burst it. A thin stream of crystal water trickled from the pipe out onto the stones. The Skorth pulled the spear away and prepared for another lunge at Eric.

"Bad move, skull guy!" Keeah yelped. She jumped behind the skeleton, while Neal and Julie raced in and rammed him from the side.

"Eeee!" the Skorth yelped as he tumbled over Julie and crashed to the stones.

Eric leaped away. "Thanks, guys!"

"Oh, man!" Neal said, sloshing in the puddle forming from the broken pipe. "I knew there would be more water. All day, it's been nothing but — *that's it*! Water! Eric, give me your socks!"

Eric blinked at him. "That's a weird request."

"GIVE ME YOUR SOCKS!" Neal cried.

Grumbling, Eric pulled off his socks and gave them to Neal, who pulled off his own red ones and stuffed them all into the broken pipe.

"The pressure is building up," said Neal. "I can feel the pipe starting to rumble. Wait till you see what happens next!"

The Skorth formed a line and charged them again.

"Everybody, scatter!" Neal shouted, holding the pipe out like a cannon. It rumbled and quaked. It trembled and quivered.

The Skorth clacked their jaws and spun their spears. They were almost on him. Neal waited.

He waited. He waited some more.

Then he tugged out the socks.

KA-SPLURSH! A powerful burst of water blasted the skeletons back.

Crash! Crunch! Clack! Skulls rolled off their necks. Toes and fingers clattered into the air. Arms and legs bounced to the cobblestones. Still the water blasted them, until the whole troop of skeletons clattered together in a heap of disconnected bones and skulls.

"The Skorth are finished!" the ghosts shouted, rushing up to the children.

Eric and his friends gasped. But it wasn't because they had defeated the Skorth. It was because of what was happening to the ghosts.

"They're . . . changing!" Julie muttered.

And they were.

As Queen Hazad hobbled over to the drawbridge, her robes suddenly shimmered

as bright as a flowery meadow. Color flowed back into her face and hands.

And not only the queen's. Every ghost's ashen skin turned hearty again. And their clothes went from gray to bright yellow, blue, and green.

"What's going on?" Neal asked.

"The day is over," said Eric, breathing heavily. "I thought —" He broke off.

A tear dripped down the queen's cheek as she laid her hand on Eric's shoulder. "The bravery you children have shown today has given us hope. We did not die in vain. Peace may come to Droon after all."

Keeah stepped forward. "We'll keep fighting until our world is free," she said.

Neal nudged Eric. "I hate to break up this party, but we have a problem."

"You mean besides our wet socks?" Eric said.

Neal held up the hourglass. There were only a few grains left in the top. "Our time is up."

Ten

Good-bye to Agrah-Voor!

"Heroes of Droon!" the queen cried. "Our hope gives us strength. Open the gate!"

The ghosts took hold of the chains and pulled on them. They were strong and hearty again. They pulled with all their might.

Errrk! The chains rattled free, the hinges squealed, and the great door lowered.

Whoom! It thudded to the ground. The

ghosts stood in awe of the opening, then gave a cheer.

"Hooray!" they boomed. "The Gate of Life is open!"

"You have given us the greatest gift," the queen said to the kids. "Thanks to you, peace may come to Droon. Thanks to you, we are lost no more. Now you must go — you cannot stay."

Eric couldn't say a word. He couldn't speak. He had a lump in his throat the size of a baseball. He wanted to cry. But they needed to go.

"Sparr has the Wasp," Keeah said.

"He does," Queen Hazad said, her cheeks becoming rosy. "It could not remain hidden forever. Yet today was a victory. Knowing there are fighters for peace like you, tonight the ghosts of Droon will sleep in hope."

"Come," said Max, scurrying onto the

drawbridge. "We must leave. Our lives are up there."

Eric nodded slowly. Together, they tramped across the bridge into the swirling fog.

Woomp! Shago swung down from the top of the wall and landed at their feet. "Julie, I believe this is yours."

He held out a bracelet with a charm on it.

"Oh, my gosh!" Julie said, glancing at her wrist. It was bare. "How did you get that?"

Shago grinned his whiskery grin as she took the bracelet from him and put it on. "I took it when we first met on the wall. You never knew."

"But I thought Sparr stole your bag?" she said.

"I stole this back when he wasn't looking. Neal, Eric, you'll need your socks."

Shago handed them to the boys. "Now I must go back. The people I love are here. They need me. And I need them."

Keeah smiled. "We'll see you again one day."

"Yes," he said. "When I follow my family into the light of Droon. Until then, farewell!"

In a flash, Shago swung back up to the top of the wall, where he stood with all the other heroes of Droon.

"For Droon!" they called down.

Whoom! The Gate of Life closed. The chains rattled for a few seconds, then became still.

"We'd better go," Eric said finally.

The fog thickened around them. They stepped carefully into it.

"I hear water," said Julie, peering down. "There's a pool here. I guess we jump in, right?"

"Of course," Neal groaned. "I mean, what would I actually *do* with dry socks?"

Keeah laughed. "Hold hands, everyone!"

Splash! As before, the instant they touched the surface, the water turned clear. A moment later, the five friends burst up through it and out onto a fresh green meadow full of colorful flowers.

Bright sunlight touched their faces.

Julie laughed. "We're out. We're alive!"

"You are indeed!" said a familiar voice.

It was Galen. He rode up on his pilka. "Welcome back to the world of the living."

"Master!" Max chirped, climbing onto Leep's back. "Did you send those snakes packing?"

Galen smiled. "We did. We won a small battle today."

Eric lowered his eyes. "We didn't do so well. Sparr got the Wasp."

Galen nodded. "The battle of Droon continues. Now come. The stairs are nearby. You must go."

Neal handed back the hourglass, and Julie gave the wizard his magic mirror.

Waving one last time to Keeah and Max, the three kids raced up the rainbow-colored stairs.

When they entered the small room at the top, they could see Keeah and Galen and Max riding off through the flowers.

Eric flicked on the ceiling light.

Whoosh! The stairs vanished and the floor appeared where the top step had been. The kids piled out of the room and into the basement. The clock on the wall told them it was the same time as when they had left.

"Eric!" Mr. Hinkle yelled from the kitchen.

"Uh-oh!" Julie gasped.

"No problem," said Eric. "The wrench is right here."

"That's not what I mean," Julie said.

"What *do* you mean?" asked Neal.

Julie stared at her wrist. "Remember the rule about not taking anything from Droon because then something from here will go there? And start a whole big mess of things going back and forth?"

Eric nodded slowly. "What about it?"

"Well, this bracelet," Julie said, pulling it off her wrist. "It isn't mine. I had a cute little fox charm on my bracelet. This is something else, some other kind of creature."

Neal breathed in sharply. He looked inside the bracelet. "Made in Droon? Uh-oh. . . ."

Eric swallowed his fear. "Back to Droon,

right away. You know what could happen —"

Thomp! Thomp! Footsteps tramped heavily down the stairs. Eric froze as his father strode into the basement.

"Dad!"

Mr. Hinkle frowned. "It took *three* of you to find a wrench? I need it to . . . to . . . ?"

Eric's father stopped and looked at his shoes. They were starting to disappear. Then his legs went invisible. Then his hands.

"Eric? What's . . . happening . . . to me?"

"Dad?" Eric mumbled. "Dad!"

A second later, his father was gone.

Neal turned white with fear. "Now your mom's going to be *really* mad!"

Eric stared at the spot where his father had vanished. "Guys . . . we'd better —"

Julie nodded. "I think so —"

"Like right now!" said Neal.

The three friends sprang to the room under the stairs . . . just as the charm on Julie's bracelet began to growl.

The
Golden Wasp*

For Jane and Lucy,
who make each day
a feast of joy and fun

Contents

One

The Moon in Droon

"Grrr! Ruff-ruff! Eeegg!"

Eric Hinkle and his best friends, Julie and Neal, jumped aside as a small dog raced across Eric's basement floor.

Except that it wasn't really a dog. It had four sharp ears, bright blue fur, a snubby pink nose, and long teeth. It growled and snarled.

And it came from another world.

A world called Droon.

"We've got to catch it, guys!" Eric cried. "We have a more serious problem, remember?"

"I'm not an *it*! I'm a moonfox!" the creature snapped. Then it bounced to the shelf above the dryer and began to chew it. *"Grrr-ruff! Ruff!"*

Julie swatted at it with a broom. "He's eating everything! We need to get him back to Droon!"

"And get my dad back *here*!" Eric cried.

Right. His dad. Mr. Hinkle.

He was the more serious problem.

Mr. Hinkle was in Droon, the strange, magical, and secret world below Eric's basement.

Droon was a world of wonder and adventure.

It was a world where an old wizard named Galen and a young princess named

Keeah battled a terrible sorcerer called Lord Sparr.

It was a world that only Eric, Julie, and Neal went to. Until now.

"I'll never go back!" the moonfox growled, scratching the window, then nibbling the frame.

Eric glanced around in a panic as his mind raced through the last twenty minutes.

He and Julie and Neal had just come back up the magical staircase that connected their world — the Upper World — to Droon. Then Julie noticed that she had left her charm bracelet behind.

And the one she wore was from Droon.

That was bad, very bad.

Galen had told them never to bring anything back from Droon. If they did, things would start going back and forth between the worlds.

And something did go. Eric's father.

First, he was here, then — *poof!* — he wasn't.

Unless they brought him back soon, other things might come here. Evil things.

Maybe even Lord Sparr himself!

Meanwhile, the charm on the Droon bracelet had come alive and was wrecking the basement.

Crunch — spah! The moonfox bit off a piece of Mr. Hinkle's tool bench, then spat it out.

"Oh, man!" Eric sighed. "What can we do?"

"Food!" yelled Neal suddenly.

"Will you *forget* food?" snapped Julie. "We have to trap this thing —"

"And food will do it!" Neal said. He dug into the seat of his favorite old armchair. He pulled out a handful of pretzels. "Good thing I'm a messy eater. Hey, moonfox, are you hungry?"

The fox screeched to a stop on a ceiling beam. "Am I *hungry*? Do I *look* hungry?"

Neal grinned. "Pretzels, here! Free pretzels!"

"Yes!" cried the fox. It jumped for the food.

In a flash, Eric grabbed a laundry basket and popped it over the fox. Julie piled some heavy cartons on top.

"I'll chew my way out!" growled the fox.

"Not before we get back!" Eric said, heading for the closet under the stairs. "Next stop, Droon. Time to find my father."

"And my bracelet," Julie added.

"And more food," said Neal as the three friends tumbled into the closet under the stairs.

Before Eric closed the door, he looked out at the basement one last time. His father's tool bench stood peacefully against the far wall. Sunlight fell through the window, flickering through the leaves of two apple trees outside his house.

Suddenly, Eric felt not just scared, but sad.

His father had taught him to climb those trees.

"He was teaching me guitar chords, too," Eric said. "I mean, what if Sparr finds him? What if somebody puts a curse on him? What if —"

"Come on, Eric," Julie whispered, pulling him into the closet. "We'll find him. We will."

Neal closed the door behind them. Julie switched off the light. The little room went dark.

Then — *whoosh!* — the floor beneath

them vanished and they were standing at the top of a long rainbow-colored staircase.

The steps shimmered in a pale light from below. It was moonlight from the land of Droon.

They stepped quickly down the stairs. They never knew where the staircase would take them, only that it would soon fade.

It always reappeared somewhere else in Droon when it was time to leave.

"I see a city," said Julie, peering down.

The moon had started to turn pale. Morning sun glinted off a giant stone palace.

Eric's heart raced when he realized where they were. "It's Jaffa City. Keeah will be here. She'll help us for sure!"

Jaffa was Droon's grand capital city. Princess Keeah lived there with her father, King Zello.

As they descended, the kids could see the palace courtyard bustling with people. Some were rushing here and there with blazing torches. Others were busily toting chests and bundles.

"Something's going on," Neal said as they left the staircase. "The whole city is out today."

Groups of six-legged, shaggy beasts called pilkas were stamping their feet near the city gates.

The sound of carriages squeaking on the cobblestones mixed with dozens of strange voices.

And one voice rang out above the others.

"Julie! Eric! Neal!"

"Keeah?" said Julie, scanning the courtyard.

"Here I am!" the princess called, waving from the crowd. Keeah wore a bright blue tunic and leggings. A jeweled crown sparkled on her long golden hair. She ran to greet the kids.

With her was her father, King Zello, a fierce-looking man in a helmet with horns sticking out of it. But he smiled when he saw the kids.

"It's a wonderful day!" Keeah said. "All the kings and queens of Droon are meeting here. We are going to Zorfendorf for a celebration. . . ."

She stopped. "Eric, what's wrong?"

"It's not a wonderful day in my world," Eric said. "Something called a moonfox is loose in my basement. Plus my dad's lost . . . in Droon."

The king's smile faded. "We must tell Galen immediately. His magic tower is nearby —"

Before they could move, a figure clad all

in black jumped from the crowd. It ran so swiftly they couldn't make out who or what it was.

"Halt, creature!" Zello cried. "Who are you?"

But the figure sprang quickly at the king. It showered a sizzling jet of red sparks over him.

Then it lurched around and leaped at Keeah.

"Get away from us!" she cried. She shot a bolt of blue light from her fingertips. The creature dodged it and bounded away across the courtyard, scattering sparks over everyone it passed.

"What's he doing?" Neal asked.

"Let's find out!" said Eric.

Together they rushed after the dark shape. It bolted through the crowd toward the city wall.

"We trapped him!" Eric shouted.

The figure ran straight for the wall, then turned around to face them. Sort of.

"Yikes!" Neal blurted out.

Eric staggered back as the creature slid into the shadows and vanished in a puff of smoke.

Keeah and Julie rushed over to the boys.

"Who was it?" asked the princess.

"I don't know," Neal said. "But he had no —"

"F-f-face!" Eric stammered. "He had no *face*!"

Two

Under a Spell

Five minutes later, the kids were climbing to the top room of the wizard's tower.

They popped through a small door and into a large round room filled with clutter.

"Hail, friends from the Upper World!" Galen boomed happily. But when they told him everything that had happened, he brooded solemnly, stroking his beard. Finally, he spoke.

"Eric, your father must be found at

once. The balance between our worlds has been upset. Julie's bracelet stayed in Droon and another went to your world. As long as Mr. Hinkle remains here, someone from Droon can ascend the stairs."

Eric shuddered. "Someone? You mean Sparr?"

The wizard nodded. "Sparr has always wanted to spread his evil reign to the Upper World. With your father here, he has his chance."

Neal gulped. "I think I speak for everyone when I say — yikes!"

"Quite," said Galen. "As for this faceless creature, I must look him up!" He pulled a thick book from a shelf.

"The kings are nearly ready!" chirped a tiny voice. The kids looked up. Max, Galen's spider troll helper, swung through the window on a thread of silk.

Max's normally wild orange hair was parted in the middle and combed down flat. His clothes were new and neat. "Master Galen, may our friends come to Zorfendorf Castle, too?"

Galen shut his book. "I'm afraid our plans have changed. Children, the faceless creature you saw is called a *wraith*."

"What's a wraith?" asked Julie.

Max gasped softly. "A wraith is a victim of the Golden Wasp. Some pour soul stung by Sparr's evil insect."

The kids stared at one another.

On their last adventure, Lord Sparr had found an object of great magic called the Golden Wasp.

Its sting gave him the power to control people's minds. Now he was using it.

For evil, of course.

Eric had a sudden, frightening thought.

"What about my dad?" he asked. "What if Sparr finds him? What if the Wasp stings him?"

The wizard narrowed his eyes. "Sparr has made it more difficult to peer into his dark lands. I suggest we find Portentia. She is a truth teller, an oracle living in the Farne Woods. If anyone knows where your father is, it is she."

Der-der! A loud trumpet fanfare sounded from the courtyard below.

"The majesties are leaving!" Max chirped. "Oh, the Lumpies will eat everything!"

Keeah rushed to the window. "Father! Father!" she called out, waving her arms.

The kids had just spotted their old friends — Khan, the purple, pillow-shaped king of the Lumpies, and Batamogi, the furry ruler of the mole people — when a second trumpet sounded.

The pilkas thundered noisily toward the gate.

"Let's hurry and get down there," said Julie.

But by the time the children made it to the courtyard, the great royal caravan had gone.

The square stood deserted.

"My father was so excited," Keeah said. "I didn't even get a chance to say good-bye."

Eric sighed. "I know what that feels like."

"Come," said Galen. "Our journey lies another way, far from Zorfendorf Castle."

They left the courtyard through a small gate.

Beyond the walls lay a broad green meadow, and on its far side, a forest of tall trees.

Galen and Max led the band across the

meadow. They traveled as quickly as they could.

"Eric, I think your father is safe," Keeah said as they neared the huge woods. "I just feel it."

"I hope so," said Eric. Just yesterday, his father helped him with his math homework. Then they played guitar together. Well, his father played, Eric mostly messed up. But it was fun.

Now he imagined waking up tomorrow without his dad at home. Tears rushed to his eyes.

"Hey, it'll be okay," said Neal, giving him a nudge. "We won't leave Droon without him."

Eric rubbed his eyes. "Um, Galen? What exactly happens if the Wasp stings you?"

The wizard turned to him. "You lose yourself, and your mind belongs to Sparr," he said. "No matter how good you are, you can be made to do bad things. After a while, you become a wraith."

Eric wanted to ask more questions, but Galen walked on in silence. The small troop continued in silence until they reached the foot of the great woods.

Everyone stopped. Julie and Neal looked at each other, then at the shadows of the forest.

"Well, what's stopping us?" Julie asked.

"Fear," said Neal. "Also fear. Plus . . . fear."

Keeah grinned. "So let's be afraid together."

The moment they stepped into the woods, the scent of pine was thick around them.

Galen and Max strode ahead. Cushions of brown needles rustled softly underfoot as they padded along. Tangled vines hung over the winding path. The kids rushed to keep up.

"Um, guys?" said Neal, ducking under a low branch. "Did I ever tell you how much I don't like dark and scary woods?"

Eric couldn't see Galen. He hurried his steps.

"Well, I don't," Neal went on. "They remind me of those creepy movies where you're walking along and suddenly —"

"Help!" Max yelped.

"It's Max! And he's in trouble," Julie cried, rushing ahead.

Two fierce, red-faced warriors had popped out of nowhere and were trying to pull Max into the bushes.

"Ninns!" Keeah yelled.

"Get away, you fiends!" Galen boomed, dashing down the path to Max. Six more large Ninns jumped from the shadows and grabbed him.

"Run!" Galen told the children. "Find Portentia! Her home is deep in the woods! Hurry!"

In a flash, a dozen more Ninns burst noisily from the bushes. "Get little ones!" they grunted.

"Let's move it!" Eric yelled.

The four children raced down the path as fast as their legs could carry them. Vines whipped their faces as they ran deeper into the woods.

Ten minutes later, out of breath, the kids stopped. Keeah raised her hand.

Everyone listened.

"No grunting, no stomping feet," said Neal. "Sounds like we lost them."

Suddenly — *kla-bamm!*

The sky exploded and the ground thundered.

The children fell to their knees. A sudden shower of hot pebbles rained over them.

Then a voice louder than the thunder boomed, "WHO D-D-DARES TO ENTER MY S-S-SACRED GR-GR-GROVE?"

Three

The Grove of Portentia

Before them stood a clearing. And at the back of the clearing sat a big gray boulder with a hole in the center.

"A talking rock?" Neal whispered. "Okay, I am out of here —"

"Don't be a scaredy-cat," said Julie.

"I see *you're* shaking," Neal retorted.

"S-S-SILENCE!" boomed the voice. As it did, another spray of pebbles spat out from the rock and fell over the grove.

"Say it, don't spray it," Julie mumbled.

"I AM P-P-PORTENTIA!" boomed the rock. "WHY HAVE YOU C-C-COME TO ME?"

Everyone looked at Eric. Quivering in fear, he stepped forward.

"We've come to ask you something," he said. "It's about —"

"SILENCE!" Portentia boomed. "First I speak, then you seek! From the dawn of time, my riddles rhyme! The secrets of Droon shall not be known soon! I speak only truth, and . . . I can . . . I shall . . . you must . . . oh, fiddlesticks!"

The stone began whispering and sputtering wildly. It sounded as if it was arguing with itself. Finally, a long sigh came from the hole.

"Oh, dear . . ."

"Portentia?" said Keeah. "Are you all right?"

"Oh, it's no use!" the stone said, spitting another tiny bit of gravel on the kids. "I try to be scary and spooky and all that. People expect an oracle to be loud and mysterious. But I don't really want to be. And *you* try rhyming all the time! Now, that's hard work!"

Julie started to laugh. Then Neal did.

Portentia began laughing, too. "Oh, I love the sound of laughter, don't you? Sounds are all I have, you know. I can't see a thing. But I sense quite a bit. And right now, I sense a boy with a problem. What can I do for you, dear?"

Eric stopped trembling. "Well, I need to know where my father is. Like me, he's from the Upper World and he's lost in Droon somewhere."

"Oh, dear, a lost father," Portentia said, sounding concerned. "And from the Upper World, too. That's not good. Is your father a king?"

Eric shook his head. "No, he's just a dad."

Portentia was silent for a moment, then said, "I see a man in plaid."

"That's the guy!" Neal shouted. "He always wears those work shirts with red and blue —"

"The man is hidden, in a city forbidden!"

Eric shivered. "Forbidden? You mean —"

"The fortress of Plud," said Portentia. "Sparr's home in the dark lands. Lots of wicked Ninns."

Eric remembered Plud from their first adventure in Droon. It was a horrible place. Dark and dreary.

"Your father is not hurt," Portentia said. "But you must find him soon."

"We will," said Eric firmly. He turned to go.

"Wait," said the oracle. "I see a bracelet. . . ."

"My bracelet!" said Julie. "That's what started it all."

"That's in Plud, too," Portentia replied. "And I also sense . . . a princess is with us?"

Keeah bowed. "I am the daughter of King Zello and Queen Relna. My name is —"

"Keeah!" Portentia cried. "Dear, dear, I knew your sweet mother. A great wizard of Droon."

The princess nodded. "She lives under a curse. I don't know where she is now."

Portentia sighed. "She has a long journey ahead, but — wait! I feel a riddle coming! A door to the past! A spell that is cast! The future of Droon is found in a tune! And, and . . . oh, well. That's all for today, I'm afraid. Most things I say don't make sense to me. Have I helped at all?"

Keeah nodded. "Yes. Thank you, Portentia."

The stone seemed to smile. "No, dear, thank *you*. I don't get many visitors. And now, for a big finish. GO! PORTENTIA HAS SPOKEN!"

Kla-bamm! Thunder clapped overhead, and one last rain of tiny pebbles splattered the kids.

They turned and made their way to the path.

"I like Portentia," Neal said as they neared the edge of the forest. "She talks like my grandma."

"I wonder what she meant," said Keeah. "'The future of Droon is found in a tune'?"

"Maybe we should all whistle," Neal said.

Eric was quiet. His father was in Plud. Sparr's fortress. Sparr's terrible, horrible home.

Keeah glanced at him, then hurried quickly along the path. "Come on," she said. "Plud is in the dark lands. We'll hurry —"

Suddenly, she stopped. She turned.

"What's wrong?" Julie asked, looking around.

"Lions?" Neal said. "Tigers? Bears? *Sparr?*"

Keeah stared into the thick trees. "The door to the past!" she said. "I . . . I . . . oh, my gosh!"

Without another word, Keeah raced deep into the forest. The three friends looked at one another.

"I guess we follow her," said Eric.

A chill wind blew swiftly through the trees.

"I guess we follow her *fast*!" cried Neal.

Four

Door to the Past

Eric, Julie, and Neal gasped when they saw it.

A cottage.

It was small and overgrown and nestled between two giant pine trees. A third tree twisted up out of the roof. A small room was built into its limbs, almost like a tree house.

"Where's Goldilocks?" Neal joked.

Julie chuckled. "If you mean Keeah, she

just went inside. Maybe we should follow her. Who knows what's in there?"

When they entered the house, Keeah was flitting around, touching everything in sight. It seemed as if she had found something that had been lost for a long time.

"What is this place?" asked Neal.

But Eric guessed. "Keeah grew up here."

"Yes!" Keeah exclaimed. "This was my home when I was small. My mother and father and I lived here for a while. I had nearly forgotten it."

Inside was a single room, neatly swept but deserted. It looked as if no one had been there for ages. A table sat in the middle, with three chairs around it. In one corner, a set of narrow stairs curved its way to the upper room in the tree.

"Oh, I had such fun here," said Keeah.

"Wow," said Neal. "Talk about a door

to the past. I guess Portentia was right about that."

"I hope she's right about my dad being safe," Eric said. "He probably won't be for long —"

"My room! My room!" Keeah said, spying the staircase in the corner and rushing to it.

She flew up the steps as if she had wings.

"I love to see her like this," Julie said.

Eric nodded. But he couldn't get his dad out of his mind. His father was in danger. And Sparr was up to something. Something big and bad.

The wind rustled noisily through the trees.

Eric went to the window. "Those Ninns are still out there. I know they are."

At home, at night, he would hear noises in the backyard. His father always took a look. It was never anything bad, just cats or something.

"We should go," he said. "Portentia told us —"

Suddenly — *plong! bling! thrum!* — strange music sounded in the upper room.

Then — *thomp! thomp!* — the ceiling quaked.

Then — "Help!"

"It's Keeah!" cried Neal, dashing up the stairs.

Keeah was backed against the bed in the tiny room. She was clutching a small, bow-shaped musical instrument. Her eyes were wide with fear. "I just touched this harp and . . . look!"

Thomp! Thomp! A metal candlestick marched heavily across the floor toward her.

Cloppety! Cloppety! A small stool had stretched its legs and was coming at her, too.

Finally, the little rug on the floor began to wrap itself tightly around Keeah's feet.

"It was my mother's harp," Keeah said. "I don't know how to play it! And I don't know what it's doing!"

Neal grabbed the rug, but it twisted away, yanking him off his feet. It jumped on him.

"Hey!" he protested. "I stand on rugs, they don't stand on me!"

The candlestick began stomping on Eric's feet.

"Ouch!" he howled. "Keeah, play something!"

"I'll try!" she said. She touched the strings.

The harp played what almost sounded like a tune. *Thrum! Bling! Pong! Bwang!*

The candlestick jerked to a halt. The stool stopped dancing. The rug fell limp on Neal.

"Whoa!" said Neal. "Good choice of tunes."

Everyone stared at the harp.

Keeah touched it again lightly. "It's called a bowharp. I had no idea it had powers."

"Maybe this is what you were supposed to find," Julie said. "'The future of Droon is found in a tune.' That's what Portentia said."

"Well, I hope dancing furniture isn't the future of Droon!" said Keeah.

"Maybe it'll help us when we get to Plud," said Neal.

Keeah smiled. "*If* I ever learn to play it."

"And *if* we ever get there," said Eric. "Can we please get going soon?"

The princess jumped to her feet. "You're right. We've stayed here long enough. Let's go."

She slung the harp over her shoulder, and they all piled out of the small cottage.

Keeah patted the door as she closed it. "I'll be back," she said. Then she turned. "Plud is in the dark lands. We have a lot of ground to cover."

"Plud," said Neal with a snort. "Take a left at No Good and head straight for Evil."

"Sounds inviting . . . not," said Julie.

Eric breathed deeply. "Let's get moving."

Without another word, the four friends headed down the path and out of the forest.

Two hours later, they started up a jagged range of steep hills. As they climbed, the ground turned darker and darker. Scattered trees stood like bony hands scratching at the sky.

The air grew smoky and foggy and foul.

"Let me guess, the dark lands?" asked Julie.

"I knew I smelled something bad," said Neal.

They crossed over a sharp ridge and stopped.

Below them stood a vast frozen lake. Next to it, a black castle. Lightning crackled overhead. Cold rain began to pelt down from the sky.

"Sparr's evil fortress," Keeah said. "Once you go in, it's hard to leave."

Eric shivered when he thought of Sparr's latest prisoner.

Five

Surprise Guests at Plud

The dark turrets and twisted towers of Lord Sparr's giant castle jutted to the sky. Troops of red-faced Ninn soldiers marched back and forth across the walls.

"Real cozy," said Julie. "Come on. Let's sneak in and out before Sparr even knows —"

Crack! A twig broke behind them.

"Ninns!" Neal gasped. In a blur of

speed, he shot up a tree. Julie jetted up right behind him.

Keeah and Eric hustled up, too. They all huddled quietly in the branches, waiting for Ninns.

But Ninns didn't come.

Hrrr! A shaggy pilka tramped over the hills toward them. On its back was a large man with a horned helmet. Behind him rode a purple, pillow-shaped creature. Next came a fox-eared king wearing a green crown.

"I can't believe it!" Keeah whispered. "It's my father. And Khan. And Batamogi! What in the world are they doing here?"

The entire procession of Droon's majesties trotted slowly up the hill.

"Maybe they're on their way to Zorfendorf?" said Julie.

Eric gaped at the procession. "But isn't Zorfendorf hundreds of miles away?"

"Yes!" Keeah said. "Father! Father! Up here!"

King Zello rode on.

"Hey, Khan!" yelled Neal. "How's it going?"

None of the majesties looked up.

"Why won't they answer?" Julie asked.

"They don't hear us," Eric said. "Or see us."

Suddenly, Batamogi burst into loud laughter.

"Shhh!" said Julie. "Plud is just over the hill!"

Then the kings broke into song.

"In Zorfendorf's bright summer sun,
We'll have our feast of joy and fun!"

"Bright summer sun?" Neal squinted at the rainy sky overhead. "Am I missing something?"

"No," said Keeah sharply. "They're imagining sunlight. They're under a spell. They've been tricked into coming here! They think that Plud . . . is Zorfendorf!"

Julie gasped. "That creepy no-face guy! Sparr sent him to shoot sparks at everyone in Jaffa City. He's the one who put the spell on them."

"If only I knew how to play this harp!" said Keeah.

Thomp! Thomp! A troop of Sparr's heavy-footed, red-faced Ninns marched after the procession, grunting to one another as they went.

The kings and queens kept singing, as if they didn't even see the Ninns.

"Why does Sparr want them?" Eric asked.

Keeah shook her head, then she began to tremble. "Oh, no! He wants to . . . to . . .

set the Wasp on them! To control their minds!"

The kids watched as the procession traveled over the hill to the fortress. Lightning flashed, and the rain came down even harder.

"We need to get down there," said Eric. "We've got a bunch of people to rescue now."

Making sure they stayed out of sight, the kids jogged quickly between the trees and down to the shore of the frozen lake.

Soon they were at Plud's rear gate. Julie crept over with Neal and pulled it open.

Inside, the thomping of Ninn feet mixed with the eerie echoes of the kings' song.

"They're going to the main court," Keeah whispered as they entered a dimly lit passage.

"Great," said Eric. "Sparr's living room."

They edged up two narrow flights of damp stairs, then along a dark hall to an open balcony.

They crouched behind the balcony railing. Below them stood a large, empty room. It was dark and cold and dreary. The walls were black.

"Okay, now what?" said Julie peering down.

"A spell spell," said Keeah, giving the kids a little smile. "I've always wanted to try one. It allows you to see what a spell is like but not be under it. Hold my hands." They did.

Then Keeah whispered, *"Empa — tempa — roo!"*

A cool, tingling sensation passed from Keeah to the others. A moment later —

Der-der! A trumpet blast announced

the guests, and a brilliant flash of light illuminated the great hall.

"Holy crow!" Eric gasped softly.

A fire blazed suddenly in the hearth. Wall torches and candles shed golden light everywhere, making the giant room bright and cheery.

"Sparr is making the place beautiful!" said Julie.

Each high wall was hung with a rich tapestry showing one of the great castles of Droon.

In between, the stones bloomed with festive holly boughs, their red berries dotting the spiky leaves like rubies.

The center of the room was filled by a long wooden table. On it were platters heaped with food and goblets brimming with drinks.

"This is exactly what Zorfendorf looks like," Keeah said. "Down to the last detail.

This must be what my father and the others are seeing."

"And here they come!" Neal announced.

Garlands of red and gold ribbons fluttered over the doors, and the majesties entered. King Zello strode in at the head of the line. Beside him walked a tall, slender, green-furred creature.

"That's Ortha, queen of the Bangledorn monkeys," Keeah whispered. "And following her is Mashta, flying empress of the sand children."

Soon the leaders of every clan and tribe in Droon were assembled in the great room.

Following them was a small army of young serving people. They carried even more platters overflowing with fruits and meats.

"I wonder if that food's real," Neal whispered.

"Ah, Zorfendorf Castle!" boomed King Zello, taking his seat near the head of the table. "My home away from home! And where is our splendid young host, Prince Zorfendorf?"

All the guests raised their silver goblets, clanked them together, and called for their host.

"Prince Zorfendorf!" the crowd cheered.

The trumpets sounded again. Everyone turned to the door. The hall rang out with louder cheers as a handsome young man entered.

"It's him!" Keeah gasped, trembling.

"How can you tell?" said Julie.

"I can tell," Neal sneered. "It's yucko himself. Lord Sparr!"

Six

The Sting of the Wasp

It *was* Sparr. But he didn't look like himself.

He appeared young and handsome. He was dressed in a bright green tunic, a red sash, and black boots. Even the weird fins that normally grew behind his ears were missing.

He grinned as he entered the hall.

"He looks like a TV star!" Julie whispered.

"Yeah," said Eric. "The star of *The Evil Show*!"

Sparr greeted his guests happily. "Kings and queens of Droon! You have come to welcome Droon's glorious summer!"

Cheers rose from the crowd. "Here! Here!"

"But first, let us welcome someone else," the sorcerer went on. "I want you to put your hands together for . . . Lord Sparr!"

The crowd went silent. Then Khan laughed. "Surely you're joking! Welcome that evil man?"

Sparr said nothing.

King Zello put down his goblet. "We will never welcome Sparr! Besides, the fiend is in Plud!"

The sorcerer grinned. "And so, my dear king, are you!" He waved his hands over the room.

Before anyone could move —

Blam! Blam! The doors slammed shut.

Sparr's own handsome face fell away to reveal his usual ugly features. His ear fins flared from purple to rich, deep red.

The bright candles and torch flames flashed, then went out. The colorful tapestries ripped into tattered black cloth, drooping on the walls.

"What is happening?" Queen Ortha cried out.

Sparr laughed as the bright green holly shriveled into weeds. The platters vanished, and in their place appeared a gold cage covered by a black cloth.

Finally, the troop of young serving people spun around and became an army of Ninn guards.

"The spell is broken," Keeah said, letting go of everyone's hands. "Everyone sees the truth."

"Free us this instant!" demanded King Zello. He reached for his sword.

Two Ninns seized the king tightly.

"Him go to dungeon? With wizard and troll and man in strange clothes?" one Ninn asked.

"Strange clothes?" Eric whispered. "My dad!"

"No, no," the sorcerer replied, smiling coldly. "I have a gift for King Zello! Wraith, come here!"

As if it took shape from the shadows themselves, the faceless wraith suddenly appeared.

"Oooh, I don't like that guy," Julie whispered.

The wraith pulled the cloth from the cage on the table. Inside was a large gold insect, humming loudly. Its sleek wings flicked rapidly on the cage walls.

"The Golden Wasp!" Keeah hissed.

"We have to get down there," Julie said.

"Not yet," the princess replied. "We're outnumbered. We need to free these prisoners first. We need all the help we can get."

"Evil creature!" King Zello shouted. "You shall not harm us!" But before he could free himself, Sparr opened the cage.

"Wasp . . . strike!" Sparr commanded.

The insect fluttered its wings and shot over to the king. Zello struggled to escape, but the Wasp struck like lightning. Its tail curled and flicked the king sharply on the forehead.

Keeah winced as her father staggered back.

"What about the harp?" asked Eric. "Can't we use its magic now?"

"I don't know what powers it has," Keeah said. "What if I make things worse?"

Suddenly, King Zello straightened up.

He broke into a big smile. "Lord Sparr!" he boomed. "How may I serve my wonderful new master?"

"This is outrageous!" Batamogi cried. He and Khan ran at Sparr. The Wasp stung them on the way. Ortha, queen of the monkeys, bounded for the door. She was stung before she reached it.

Again and again, the Wasp attacked, until all the royalty of Droon had been stung.

Together, they stared at Lord Sparr.

Together, they bowed before him.

Together, they spoke in one voice.

"What would make you happy, Lord Sparr?"

The sorcerer cast his fiery eyes over the crowd. "In a room far below, I have some *gifts* for you. You will take them back to your own countries."

"Gifts, huh?" whispered Neal. "Something tells me they won't be fun."

"But there is more, my slaves!" Sparr went on. "In my dungeon down below is a man from the Upper World. As long as he is here, I can ascend the stairs. With your help, I shall conquer Droon. With *his* help, I shall conquer the Upper World! Yes, my slaves! I . . . shall take his place!"

Eric nearly choked. "What? What? That . . . that can't happen! Take . . . his . . . *place?*"

The majesties of Droon cheered over and over.

"Eric . . ." Keeah's hand was on his shoulder. Her eyes were moist, but she managed a smile. "It won't happen, I promise. Let's go find him. And Max. And Galen."

"And my bracelet," said Julie. "It's up to us to get things back to normal."

"Yeah," said Neal. "Before Sparr starts moving his stuff into your basement!"

But as Keeah pulled them along, Eric feared that nothing would ever be normal again.

Quietly, they hurried down the stairs.

To the dungeon.

Seven

The Locked Room

They entered a dark tunnel under the fortress.

With each step, Eric felt himself drawing closer to his father. He was here. Eric could feel it.

"I say we find the prisoners first," said Keeah. "Then the bracelet. I don't want us to split up."

Julie nodded. "Good idea."

"We should follow our noses," said Neal. "The dungeon's gotta smell the worst."

Eric winced. Neal was probably right. He wondered how his father was handling being in Droon. He sure wasn't seeing the best part of it.

As they went deeper into the dark passage, they heard a faint droning sound in the distance.

Nnnn. Nnnn. It sounded like a motor.

"Weird place," Eric said. "But I definitely think we're getting close."

"Close? We're here!" Neal said. He pointed to a door with a sign over it.

The sign read DUNGEON.

Julie laughed. "Nice of Sparr to label things."

"He probably had to, so the Ninns wouldn't get lost," Keeah said with a smile.

Together, they pulled open the heavy door.

They stepped into a room lit by the dim glow of a single wall torch. Eric spied three figures in chains. None of them was moving.

"Please let one of them be my dad," he said softly. "And please let him be okay."

They edged closer.

"It's called plaid," one voice said. "It comes in lots of colors. You can even get plaid pants!"

"Is that so?" said another excitedly. "I've seen the pattern before, but I can't re-member where!"

"I wonder if I can weave plaid with my spider silk," chirped the third. "It looks quite soft."

Eric stepped into the light. "Um . . . hello? Dad?"

"Eric!" cried his father, his face beam-ing. "Holy crow! Why didn't you ever tell

me about this Droon place? And right under our house!"

"Ah," said Galen cheerfully. "Our rescuers have arrived. I told you, Sir Hinkle. They would never fail us."

Eric blinked at his father. "*Sir* Hinkle?"

Max rattled his eight chains. "Not exactly the feast of joy and fun we were all expecting!"

"Now, Keeah," said Galen. "A number-two blue bolt should release us. I would have done it myself, only the angle wasn't right. I didn't want to zap us all to Agrah-Voor!"

Keeah raised her hands and narrowed her eyes. "Stand back!" she said. A sudden bolt of blue light shot neatly from her fingertips.

Kzzz-zamm! The chains crumbled into a dusty heap on the floor. The prisoners were free.

Eric hugged his father. It felt strange to do that in front of his friends, but it felt good, too. Things were getting back to normal. Sort of.

Neal told Galen what was happening. "Sparr's Wasp stung all the majesties. Now he's sending them back to conquer their countries for him."

"And I need to find my bracelet right away," said Julie. "Sparr will probably use it to keep the door open so he can get to the Upper World."

Neal nodded. "There isn't a room marked BRACELET around here, is there?"

Mr. Hinkle blinked. "Almost! I think we passed a sign that said LOCKED ROOM. Galen, do you think maybe Sparr is keeping the bracelet there? Galen?"

But the wizard's eyes were fixed on Keeah's harp. "Forgive me," he said, a smile creeping over his lips. "I had thought that old harp was lost forever. It makes me happy to see it. Droon's ancient past lives again. It gives me much hope."

Keeah made a face. "Except that I can't play."

Galen nodded. "You will, Princess, when the time is right. Now, come. We are wasting time."

They left the dungeon.

Five minutes later they stood before a tall iron door set into the stone. The door had a huge padlock on it and a sign that read LOCKED ROOM.

Nnnn. The droning was loud behind the door.

"What's Sparr got cooking in there?" Neal wondered out loud.

Galen turned to Keeah. "Pluck the third string of the harp."

The princess did. *Brum!*

Ploink! The lock popped off, and the door sprung open.

"It does work!" Keeah said, beaming.

The room inside seemed to glow. The walls narrowed to a point at the ceiling.

And the droning was even louder.

Julie gasped. "It's here!"

The bracelet — her silver charm bracelet — was sitting alone on a tall stand in the center of the room. She darted over to it.

"It's strange that no one is guarding it," said Keeah.

Eric looked around. Up and down the walls were thousands of little holes, all exactly the same size. And the humming was coming from all around them. "I'm not so sure. . . ."

Julie took the bracelet from the stand and slipped it on. "Yes! It's mine! Things will be normal again, I know they will."

Something moved in one of the holes.

The humming grew louder.

"What was that?" said Mr. Hinkle.

Eric stepped over to him. "I saw it, too."

Something else moved. Galen edged closer.

Zzzt! A tiny golden object shot out of a hole and buzzed around his head. He swatted at it. It buzzed back into its hole.

The humming grew still louder.

Then Galen knew. They all knew. He staggered backward. "Oh, dear, no!" he cried. "We're in . . . we're in . . . a nest!"

The walls were suddenly alive. The holes swarmed with thousands of tiny wasps.

"These must be the children of the Golden Wasp," Galen said, pulling the kids toward the door. "Sparr set them to guard Julie's bracelet."

Eric's eyes gaped. "Sparr said he was giving the kings gifts to help them conquer their countries. These wasps . . . are the gifts!"

Galen's face flashed with fear and anger. "We must stop him. Quickly, children, find the kings. Take them to safety!"

"But Sparr has them under his control!" Julie said. "They'll do only what *he* says!"

The wizard turned to Keeah. "Princess, you are your mother's daughter. I had not thought it possible, but you have found her lost harp. You must learn its power before you are truly ready. But it may be our only hope against Sparr."

Keeah looked at her mother's old harp.

Galen took her by the shoulders. "Go into the depths of your mind and bring up the memory of what she played to you.

Only love can conquer Sparr's evil. Only you can defeat him today. Go! Save your father. Save Droon!"

Keeah looked into the wizard's eyes. All of a sudden, they seemed very old.

"But what about you?" she asked.

"I must stay here. I have business to do. Go!"

Mr. Hinkle and Max rushed the kids out of the room. Galen slammed the door behind them.

Lightning crackled from inside the room.

The humming grew louder.

Eight

Sparr's Wicked, Wicked Plan

The rain was even colder when they snuck into the outer courtyard. They hid behind a row of barrels and peered over.

Lord Sparr was on a high wall, looking down.

Below him, the majesties of Droon stood smiling blankly up at him.

"Ninns!" the sorcerer boomed. "Let us begin!"

A long line of his warriors tramped into the courtyard. Each one held an empty golden cage.

"Go, my soldiers!" Sparr cried. "Fill your cages with the children of the Wasp! Then you shall bring my gifts to every land in Droon!"

Saluting, the Ninns trudged into the fortress.

"So it's true," whispered Keeah. "Sparr is sending those wasps back with the kings. Then every good soul in Droon will belong to Sparr!"

Mr. Hinkle scanned the courtyard. "I don't know much about Droon, but this looks bad."

"It *is* bad, Sir Hinkle," said Max. "*Very* bad."

Eric wasn't sure they could do anything to stop Sparr. But he knew they had to try.

He turned to Keeah. "Galen said you need to remember the songs your mother played."

Keeah shook her head. "It seems so long ago. I don't remember anything."

"Yeah, my dad teaches me songs, too," Eric replied. "Sometimes I forget. Then I just start playing. It helps me remember."

Sparr mumbled a word, and his wraith slithered from a dark corner and stood next to him.

"Well, King Zello," the sorcerer called down, "how do you like serving me?"

"I love it!" the king boomed up happily.

"Good!" Sparr replied. "For soon you'll end up like my wraith here. A mere shadow!"

Keeah growled with anger, then closed her eyes. "Mother, help me to remember."

A moment later, a red-faced Ninn charged out of the fortress. "F-F-F."

Sparr snarled at him. "Well? What is it?"

"F-FIRE!" the Ninn cried. "Nest on fire!"

Thick smoke poured up suddenly from below.

Sparr flew down from the wall. "No! My glorious plan must not fail! Ninns, follow me to the nest. Wraith — summon your brothers!"

Eric gulped. "That thing's got . . . *brothers?*"

Sparr roared into the fortress. His red-faced guards chugged noisily after him as the wraith vanished back into the shadows.

"Now's your chance, Keeah," said Julie.

The princess looked over at her father. Then she looked at her friends and nodded firmly.

Lifting the harp, she began to play.

Bling! Thrum! Bimm! Keeah's fingers

moved magically over the strings as if she suddenly remembered an old song. She played more and more as the sound swirled around the courtyard.

Blim! Ping! Bong! Thoom!

The majesties of Droon began to stir. They blinked once. Then again. They looked around. Then they began to mumble to one another.

"The kings are themselves again," Max said.

"The spell is broken!" Julie exclaimed. "Keeah, you did it!"

King Zello turned as if awakened from a deep sleep. He gasped to see his daughter there. And he gasped when he saw the high black walls of the fortress. "Keeah . . . where are we?"

The princess rushed to her father and hugged him. "We're in Plud, Father. But we must all leave now. Quickly, this way! To the gate!"

Mr. Hinkle dashed over to help. "Hi, I'm Eric's dad. I think we'd better move out fast. That Sparr guy is mad we're messing up his plans."

King Zello slapped Eric's father on the shoulder. "Good to have your help, Sir Hinkle! Majesties of Droon, let's go!"

Neal nudged Eric. "Look at that. King Zello and Sir Hinkle. Two cool dads."

"Yeah," said Eric proudly. "Very cool!"

"Our problems aren't over yet," said Keeah.

Zzzt! The Golden Wasp shot out from the fortress. It looked mad. It sounded mad.

"Uh-oh, I think it's mad!" Eric yelled.

Neal threw a stone at it. The Wasp buzzed in a circle, then stopped. It looked at Neal. Then it flicked its wings rapidly. Then it shot after him.

"It's mad, all right," said Neal. "At me!"

Neal took off as the Wasp chased him into the burning fortress.

The kids stared at one another.

"After him!" they yelled.

Nine

Fire and Ice

"Help! Help! *Hellllllp!*"

Neal's cries for help echoed in the dark halls.

Eric, Keeah, and Julie rushed after him until they reached the main court.

The Wasp had Neal backed into a corner.

"You're trapped!" said Eric, looking around.

"You think?" Neal shouted. "Do something!"

The Wasp hovered over Neal. Its tail twitched near his face. The long stinger waved back and forth in front of his nose. It came closer, closer.

Keeah ran over. Blue sparks shot off the tips of her fingers. "Neal — duck!"

"Looks like a big insect to me!" Neal said.

"Get down!" she shouted. He did.

Kla-bamm! Keeah's shot of blue light blasted the Wasp. It was thrown into the wall behind Neal.

ZZZZT! The Wasp was up before they left the room. The kids raced through dark halls, down stairs, and along dim passages.

They stumbled and ran and ran and stumbled until they could run no more.

Suddenly, it wasn't dark anymore. The walls of the passage glowed yellow and red.

"The nest!" Julie gasped, peering ahead.

The wild humming of the other wasps was nearly drowned out by the roar of the fire. Red, yellow, and blue flames licked the ceiling of the room Galen had set on fire.

Zzzzt! The Golden Wasp saw the burning nest, gave out a shriek, and shot in over the kids.

Inside the nest, Galen stood facing Sparr and his troop of Ninns. The wizard narrowed his eyes. "Your plan is finished, evil one! Give up!"

"Too late," the sorcerer snarled. "My plan has already begun. The strangers shall not leave Droon. Even now the stairs appear in my dark lands. I will ascend them. You cannot stop me."

Keeah ran in and stood next to Galen. "Oh, I think you'll be surprised —"

Sparr let out a long hissing noise. "Ah,

the princess. Good. Now you can perish together!"

Kla-bamm! He hurled a red lightning bolt at them. Galen and Keeah twirled out of the way.

At the sound of the blast, the Ninns bolted past the kids, scurrying for cover.

"Children, go!" Galen called out. "We will meet you outside!"

"But, Keeah —" Julie said.

"I'll be all right," the princess said with a smile. She tapped her harp. "Now, go!"

Kla-bamm! Sparr leveled another blast. Keeah blocked it with one of her own. The room lit up.

"We better get out of here!" Neal yelped.

The three friends charged through the passage and up the stairs. They tumbled out to the main courtyard where Mr. Hinkle and Max were waiting for them.

"The stairs are across the lake!" Max said.

Eric turned around. All of Plud was on fire.

Black smoke rose up, then fell over the lake.

"It's like the end of the world," Neal said. "And I'm not ready!"

"We need to go now!" Max said, running for the gate.

Eric shook his head. "I have this weird feeling we've forgotten something."

"I have my bracelet," said Julie.

"And you have me!" said Mr. Hinkle.

"Come, Eric," Max said, pulling the children gently out the gate. "Galen and Keeah will be fine. Together they are more powerful than Sparr. Keeah proved that today. Now, come."

The flames roared higher and higher as they all ran to the shore. King Zello and the others were already halfway across the ice. The magic staircase stood glistening on the far side.

The kids started across the lake. They were nearing halfway when Eric stopped. He turned around.

A wall of black smoke was rolling across the ice toward them. Eric stared at it. He listened.

"Son, what is it?" his father asked.

"I just remembered what we forgot," said Eric.

A sound was coming from behind the smoke.

Sloosh . . . sloosh . . .

It was the sound of metal on ice.

Suddenly, there it was. The wraith. It burst out from the smoke and skated toward them.

Sloosh . . . sloosh . . .

It was joined by another. Then another.

And another. An army was skating toward them.

"Mr. No-face . . . and his brothers," said Julie.

"I think we better move it," said Neal.

Eric nodded. "I think . . . you're right!"

Ten

The Harp and the Wasp

The kids tore across the ice, slipping and sliding toward the glittering staircase.

"We're never going to make it," Max chittered. "The wraiths are too fast!"

Suddenly — *ka-whoom!*

Plud's highest tower exploded into bits.

"Oh, my gosh!" Julie cried. "Keeah! Galen!"

Then — *whoosh! whoosh!* — Galen flew out of the flaming fortress. Behind him, Keeah was flying, too. She held her harp in front of her. It was pulling her swiftly through the air.

"Awesome!" Eric exclaimed. "They made it!"

"So did *they*!" Neal said, pointing to two dark streaks zooming across the sky.

The black flaps of Sparr's long cloak glistened like crow wings as he swooped after Keeah. The Golden Wasp followed close behind.

"Come, wraiths! Come, Ninns!" Sparr called out. "We will all ascend the stairs!"

Kla-bamm! His angry blast struck the sky near the wizards. Keeah was thrown down through the air. She tumbled to the lake near the kings.

Her father scooped her up instantly, but the harp struck the ice, bounced, and slid away from her. "Don't let Sparr get it!" Keeah cried out.

Eric dashed over and snatched up the harp. It seemed to hum in his hands. He knew instantly: *There is power in this harp.*

"Come, wraiths!" Sparr howled. "Onward, Ninns! Don't let them get to the stairs!"

Sloosh! Sloosh! The wraiths skated closer. The Ninns charged across the ice.

"We need a spell to stop them," said Julie.

"Keeah and Galen have their hands full with Sparr," Neal said, looking around wildly.

Eric stared at the harp in his hands. He turned to his father and held it out to him. "Play this, Dad."

"What?" his father said, shaking his head. "This is magic. I can't do magic. I'm just a dad."

"You taught me chords," said Eric. "You

taught me lots of stuff. You have to play it! Or Sparr will get into our house. Our world!"

Sloosh! The wraiths were racing over the ice.

Mr. Hinkle looked at Eric, then took the harp. "Here goes nothing." He touched the strings.

Plong! Ploink! Bloing! Plinkkkk!

"I thought you could play!" Neal groaned, slapping his hands over his ears. "That hurts!"

Suddenly, *kkkk!*

A crack appeared in the ice. It widened. The frozen lake split into dozens of pieces.

"Whoa, Mr. H.," said Julie. "You *can* play!"

The wraiths slid to a stop at the edge of the crack. They could go no farther.

The Ninns weren't so lucky.

"Argh! Ooof!" *Splash!*

The clumsy, red-faced warriors crashed into one another. Then they plopped into the icy water.

"Dad, you did it!" Eric shouted. "You did it!"

"To the stairs! Quick!" Keeah yelled, running over to them. They all skittered across the ice and bolted up the bank to the waiting stairs.

Kla-bamm! Galen fired a bolt of light at Sparr, stunning him, then joined the kids on the stairs. Together they ran to the room at the top.

Sparr leaped desperately after them, howling, "The Upper World is mine. Strike, Wasp, strike!"

"Here, Keeah," said Mr. Hinkle, handing her the harp. "It's time to do your stuff."

The Golden Wasp shot toward Keeah.

"Princess, prepare to become mine!" Sparr cried, climbing up after them. "Wasp — strike!"

Keeah stood firmly on the stairs, the cold wind blowing around her. She touched the strings.

Eric knew at once. The melody she played came from somewhere deep in her memory.

"Wasp — strike her!" Sparr cried again.

The Wasp did strike. It struck quickly.

But not at Keeah.

For an instant, it hovered over her, entranced by the melody she was playing. Then it lowered its tail and shot over to Sparr.

"Away! Away!" the sorcerer shouted.

But the Wasp would not obey him. It swept in and stung him — *ZZZZZZT!*

The sorcerer gasped, clutching his forehead. "No! No! The Upper World belongs to me. I must — must — *akkkgh*!"

Sparr howled angrily as he plummeted — half flying, half falling — to the frozen lake below.

Eric trembled all over, staring at the sorcerer.

Sparr lay thrashing on the ice, yowling and roaring as his Ninns slid across the lake to him.

Behind him, the black fortress of Plud was red with flame.

"It is over, for now," Galen said. "Come. . . ."

Eric stared at the ice below. Even from that far away it seemed as if Sparr's fiery eyes were glaring at him. Piercing right to his heart.

It is not over.

That's what those eyes told him.

Julie tugged Eric to the top of the stairs. "The moonfox broke out. He's making another mess."

Eric ran through the closet into the basement.

Sunlight shone in as it had when they left.

"Holy cow!" Mr. Hinkle cried. "What a mess!"

The moonfox had eaten its way out of the laundry basket. Now it was tearing the stuffing out of the old chair.

"Hey, that's where I sit!" Neal yelled.

"I'll take care of him," Galen said, lurching into the basement with Keeah. He stared at the creature and thrust out his hands.

"Zof — kof — peechu — meechu — mack!"

The moonfox turned to Galen with his mouth full of stuffing. "Wait, no —"

Bloink! He vanished in a puff of green air. In his place, a gold charm bracelet clattered to the basement floor.

Max scampered over, snatched the Droonian bracelet, and dropped it into a pouch on his belt.

He beamed. "And that's that!"

"Hooray!" Julie cried. "It's over!"

Everyone breathed a sigh of relief.

Mr. Hinkle just stood staring at the whole thing. "Boy, Eric, wait till I tell your mother."

Galen smiled. "That reminds me. Sir Hinkle?"

"Yes, Galen?"

"Somban — romban — toop!"

Eric's father gave a sudden wiggle, then a giggle, then he stared ahead. Then his eyes slammed shut. And he started humming.

"Your father is forgetting everything that happened to him," Galen said to Eric. "Droon must remain a secret known only to the chosen ones."

"Chosen ones?" said Neal. "I like that."

Eric sighed. He knew Galen was right.

"Sorry, Dad," he said softly. "It was fun."

Mr. Hinkle coughed, then sneezed, then his eyes popped open. "Um . . . what just happened? I mean . . . where . . . um . . . what . . . Oh, never mind! Just clean up this mess, will you?"

"Yes, sir!" said Julie.

Mr. Hinkle turned. "For some reason, I like when you call me *sir*." Then he tramped upstairs, scratching his head.

"Galen, we'd better leave now," Keeah said to the wizard. She headed to the closet, then turned and smiled at Eric. "Once again, you have —"

Keeah glanced behind him. Her eyes widened suddenly. She pointed out the basement window at the trees outside. She began to tremble.

"What's wrong?" Julie asked.

"Those trees —" she said.

"Apple trees," Eric said. "My dad taught me how to climb on those trees."

Keeah stared at the sun winking through the bright green leaves of the twin trees.

"I've . . . been here . . . before," she said.

Eric felt as if lightning had struck him. "What? What? But . . . how is that *possible*?"

"I don't know," Keeah said. "I . . ."

"Hurry!" Max called from the closet. "The stairs are fading. We must not stay!"

Keeah turned to the wizard. "Galen,

could this be true. Could I have been here before?"

He pulled Keeah gently to the stairs. "All things are possible. But this is a mystery for another day. Come, Princess, we must leave here!"

He rushed into the closet with Keeah and Max.

Eric ran in and looked down as the three of them sped down the stairs and into the pink sky.

Keeah kept looking back until she disappeared into the clouds below.

Julie and Neal stood next to Eric, holding the door open until the stairs faded completely.

No one spoke for a long time. Finally, Eric flicked on the light in the closet.

Whoosh! The floor appeared. Droon vanished.

Eric turned to his friends. "What Keeah said . . . It's impossible, right?"

Neal restuffed the chair and slumped down into it. "Been here before? I mean . . . when?"

Julie bit her lip and shook her head. "Talk about secrets? You guys, that's gotta be Droon's biggest one yet!"

Eric nodded. "Something tells me we're just beginning to discover the real secrets of Droon."

"And you know what that means?" said Neal. "Lots more adventures!"

Eric smiled. Adventures. That sounded good.

He turned to his friends. Then he glanced out the basement window to the yard outside.

"Hey, guys, who feels like climbing a tree?"

"I do!" said Neal, springing up from the chair.

"Me, too!" said Julie, jumping ahead of him.

Eric joined them on the stairs as they raced out to the backyard to play.

ABOUT THE AUTHOR

Tony Abbott is the author of more than three dozen funny novels for young readers, including the popular *Danger Guys* books and *The Weird Zone* series. Since childhood he has been drawn to stories that challenge the imagination, and like Eric, Julie, and Neal, he often dreamed of finding doors that open to other worlds. Now that he is older — though not quite as old as Galen Longbeard — he believes he may have found some of those doors. They are called books. Tony Abbott was born in Ohio and now lives with his wife and two daughters in Connecticut.